I0728215

WHEN LOVE GETS *Better*

Imogene Grant

Zeta Publishing

Ocala, FL

Zeta Publishing, Inc
3850 SE 58th Ave
Ocala, FL 34480
www.zetapublishing.com

This is a work of fiction. All of the characters, names, incidents, organizations, and dialogue in this novel are either the products of the author's imagination or are used fictitiously.

Ordering Information:
Quantity sales. Special discounts are available on quantity purchases by corporations, associations, and others. For details, contact the publisher at the address above.
Orders by U.S. trade bookstores and wholesalers. Please contact Zeta Publishing: Tel: (352) 694-2553; Fax: (352) 694-1791 or visit www.zetapublishing.com

ISBN: 978-1-947191-68-6 (sc)
ISBN: 978-1-947191-69-3 (e)

Library of Congress: 2018937816
Printed in the United States of America

Chapter 1

◆

In buildings everywhere, above the heads of the general public as in Los Coronado, California a short distance outside Los Angeles. Ordinary human beings work for the wealthiest CEO's and presidents of big business who are most probably fifty-ish, brilliant, and distinguished to look upon. They rule over board meetings, holding conferences by telephone, or by any means they dean necessary. We'll seldom see them, nor the offices or businesses they control, except on television. This symbol of power can touch a button and a secretary will materialize along with several alternate executives. One after another will file in and take their places at the conference table. The commands to sell this or that, fire thus in so, take over these businesses, make appointments, and it goes on unerringly. When all assignments are made, this paragon of power asks, "Anymore business?"

Conference over, the CEO tells his secretary while she trots behind him that he is on his way to the airfield. Her job is to call his home and have his wife meet him there. Then call the airport and make sure his plane will be ready promptly within the hour as she struggled to follow his long strides, his instructions continue, "If Mr. So-in-so should call, put him through to me in the limousine. If not I will get back to him in seventy-two hours. Make my excuses to the Senator for Wednesday; and those business people who count the most, and you know who they are, tell them I will be back on Thursday."

Benton Cavanaugh was good looking but not as tall as most of his friends, and he had a tendency to gain weight with most small indulgencies. William Jordan on the other hand was tall and lean, he wore his clothes no matter what, with elegance. They swore to be ,friends for life as they grew up in the nineteen forties. Their ancestral backgrounds were similar, from old money. The young men attended the same prep school and eventually went to the University together where they were inseparable. Side by side at eating contests, drinking competitions, and they got drunk just for the hell of it. Partying to excess, engaging in panty raids, one, almost flunked his junior year; both toured Europe on a shoestring after graduation. They loved as brothers and at times were closer than most siblings, never a disagreement.

William was well read, professional to a degree, his brilliance was noted by his persistence. Their first mistake was, when they went into business together. Lucrative deals went sour and they lost thousands of dollars.

Benton on the other hand, became a hot-tempered tightwad and held a dollar until the eagle screamed. Actually, he was like his father even though his family was well off. He was ingenious in business affairs, and had his suspicions of William's laid back manner toward money.

Benton stormed into his old friends' office one cold winter afternoon; "You're a scoundrel, William Jordan!" He bellowed.

"What's wrong?" William asked.

"This has happened too many times to be a mistake!" as he shook a packet of papers in the air.

"If you will calm down and tell me what you're talking about, maybe I can answer intelligently,?" William asked.

"You won't get another chance to swindle me again!" Benton fumed angrily.

William sat toying with his pen…Benton never gave him a chance to explain, but whirled around and slammed out.

Twenty plus years passed between 1970 to the late nineteen nineties while William and his wife Patricia built a palatial home in the hills just far enough away from town where a clear stream meandered through the back of the property.

Each family lived on opposite ends of upscale affluent sections of Los Coronado.

The Jordan settings were tranquil with the natural beauty of its surroundings. The hilly landscape was dotted with the shade of serene ancient trees, and flowering plants. All rooms of the mansion faced a portion of the picturesque sights. Terraced gardens and lawns were carefully tended along with the sunken tennis courts. Indoor Olympic heated swimming pool, with hot tub and spa. The master plan of the home was thoughtfully designed. The inside was extraordinary, there was a feeling of old England tucked in a secluded niche at the end of a private road. Including a Royal master suite featuring luxurious bathrooms and sitting room with a romantic fireplace, a sumptuous kitchen with butler's pantry, and formal dining room. There was a ballroom living room along with an ample family entertainment area.

The gardens were arranged with red roses from the house of Lancaster. The white roses of the house of Yorkshire and other flowering plants burst into a kaleidoscope of colors.

Benton Cavanaugh retaliated by buying his acreage in a secluded area outside the city with a private lane. His architect was brought over from England to design his and Connie's home.

His wife paid infrequent attention to her husbands' episodes of rage. Actually she loved him dearly, and was always aware that his bark was worse than his bite.

The Cavanaugh home was a variety of English Gothic, while under the Tudor's of England distinguished by flat centered arches, shallow moldings and a lavishness of paneling on the walls done in perpendicular style. A designer pool house and spa was enormous and accented by a cool, special stone decking. The inside was extraordinary; with the feeling of old England tucked in a secluded niche at the end of a private road.

Their competition was fierce over the years, in business as well as their personal lives. Each considered the other to be his archenemy; and their names were never mentioned in the others home again.

Their children went to separate schools and Paige Cavanaugh was sent to Europe.

The Jordan's son attended prestigious eastern schools.

Growing up the children seldom saw each other, except in passing, family vacations were spent on separate continents. Their feuding was done almost exclusively in business and in the news media.

Anthony Jordan, William's son had a volatile temper and had achieved success on the tennis circuits around the world, and especially the United States Open. He was a promising young man to win at Wimbledon.

Paige Cavanaugh, Benton's daughter, while in Switzerland had written a bestselling novel that was unique in Europe. The hardback was being introduced in the United States. Her book signing ceremony took place at Galbert's Contemporary books.

These young people knew of one another and the family feud, but traveled in different circles.

Today after all the years in between the mirrored walls of the elevator reflected the anger on Benton Cavanaugh's aging face. Fuming, he glared at the news headlines then slapped the folded newspaper against his thigh repeatedly. Benton was of average height, his body had softened, and his portly girth had expanded, he was losing the battle to hide it. He angered almost to apoplexy if crossed. Seething, his normally ruddy complexion was even more red, if that were possible. In spite of those shortcomings, he was an astute, intelligent industrialist whose business decisions were sound.

When the elevator stopped at his floor, he charged out into the hall past the other passengers, Benton stormed down the hall to the door inscribed with Jordan Enterprises. where he slammed through the door into the outer office, striding angrily down the aisle, passing astonished office workers.

William's secretary closest to the door marked private tried to stop Benton from entering the office.

"Sir! Sir! You can't go in there!" she hurried to stand in front of him, saying, "Sir! Sir! Sir you can't go in there!" Trying to prevent him opening the door, but

Benton moved her aside and threw the door open wide.

William, Jordan sat behind his desk, lean and refined. He looked up as the door burst open; his secretary stood helplessly by. He signaled to her his understanding, and she was reluctant to close the door.

The leather of his chair creaked softly when he leaned back.

"You're a damn crook! You'll never get away with this!' Benton barked furiously, his face engorged with blood.

"De 'ja vu, isn't this the way we parted over twenty years ago?" William said.

"I read about that Cartel business too! That makes you a bigger rogue!" Benton said, shaking his finger in William's face.

"Well, hello Benton, I see your vocabulary hasn't changed since then." William said coolly civil.

"Don't you hello me! You, you barefaced degenerate! You, you troublemaker!" he responded, pointing to the headlines.

William looked at the front page; Jordan Enterprises take over a subsidiary of Cavanaugh the conglomerate.

"Oh that," William laughed.

Benton drew himself up to his full five feet ten inch height and made a futile effort to hold in his abdomen. "We'll meet in court! I'll break you for everything you're worth!" he said.

William stood and leaned on his desk, saying, "Let me explain. It was a package deal and this happened to be in it, I optioned that before you.. I didn't go searching for your, little company! Go on take me to court," he roared, slapping his palm on the newspaper.

"A likely story, you had a hand in this! Once a crook, always one!" Benton sputtered, shaking his fist in William's face.

"Somebody fell asleep over at Cavanaugh or else how did this little company fall through the cracks?" he asked knowing how to push Benton's buttons, and grinned his voice loaded with sarcasm.

The office staff looked on in nervous surprise.

"You deserve a beating! I'll wipe that grin off your stupid face!" Benton shouted.

"Take your best shot! You overblown windbag! Don't hurt yourself you portly jackass!" William scoffed.

Benton slapped him across the face.

In the background there was a sharp intake of collected breaths from the Jordan staff.

William came from behind his desk and slugged Benton in the eye.

A horrified secretary stepped aside to let the security guards in. Benton was dragged away by the guards, he shouted, "You're a con artist, just like your father!" he struggled to break away. "You'll be sorry! If our families meet don't speak! I'll fix you!" then to the guards, "Let me go! You overgrown lummoxes!" and struggled with the security guards who had to literally carry him through the door, his feet touching the carpet at times.

William brushed imaginary dust from the lapels of his jacket, then sat behind his desk. He looked up to find his staff watching him in awe. "Thanks Kim, the show is over you can all go back to work now." He instructed with cosmopolitan charm.

The group went away and Kim closed the door.

In the back seat of Benton's limousine, his eye was an angry red and his cheek had begun to swell. He touched it gingerly, grimacing in pain. "That obstinate, churlish, jackass! I'll show him!" he grumbled.

"Can I get something for your eye, sir? An ice pack, maybe?" the chauffeur asked in a droll tone of voice.

"No! Just get me home!" Benton answered with ill temper.

The chauffeur steered the automobile into the flow of traffic, and at times looked in the rearview mirror at his employer and fought to hold back a grin.

That night, Paige Cavanaugh who had intelligence and wit, with beauty and grace. She had resources in her own right but felt stifled at times.

Dinner with Ashley Boregard-Smith for the evening was over. He was acceptable to Benton who considered him a no nonsense older man for his daughter. One that would keep her in line if need be, even though Ashley was only thirty five he seemed more mature.

Ashley was formally ceremonious, handsome and sedately elegant, a holier than thou snob.

As they left the dining room he stopped momentarily beside the Madre D', who said, "Have a good evening, sir."

"Excellent dinner, Carl. The service was beyond reproach as usual," Ashley replied, tucking a generous tip in the Madre D's palm.

Paige nodded as they left the restaurant.

In the limousine they sat in composed silence while the driver maneuvered the sleek car smoothly through traffic.

Ashley sat and looked at her lovely profile, "Do you have plans for tomorrow?" he asked.

"Lunch with June, then work on my screenplay," she answered turning toward him as the city lights moved behind her in a kaleidoscope of colors.

"I have to fly to Europe," he said.

"Oh Ashley, why?" She asked.

"Some difficulty with Smith Industries there. Don't worry your pretty head about it, dear," he said taking her hand in his.

"Will it take long?" Paige asked.

"No, I expect it should take a week at the most," he paused a moment, then said, "I'll be back in time for the symphony."

"I'll miss you," she said.

He drew her close and Paige rested her head on his well-tailored shoulder. "That will all be over soon, dear. After we're married you'll be with me where ever I go," he said softly as they arrived at the Cavanaugh home.

The chauffeur went around the car to open the rear door.

Ashley said to the driver, "I'll just be a moment."

The chauffeur waited while Ashley walked Paige to the front door. He faced her, saying, "We can enjoy tomorrow evening. Have dinner with me and see me off at the airfield."

"Eight o'clock?" she asked.

He held her shoulders between his manicured hands. "Dinner was excellent and you made it so, as always," he said.

Their bodies touched momentarily when he lightly touched her lips with a sterile kiss."I'll call you tomorrow," Ashley said, before returning to the limousine.

The chauffeur closed the door and walked around to the driver's side and drove away.

She stood watching while the automobile disappeared into the street before she went slowly inside. Paige sighed, saying, "I hope this relationship becomes more passionate after the marriage."

Passing the sumptuous living room she saw her parents were still awake.

Connie was reading a book and Benton was noisily folding the pages of the paper Money Maker Daily.

"Oh Mom, Dad I'm glad you're awake," Paige said.

Connie Cavanaugh was a gracious woman, well coifed and cared for. She did her share of things society and her husband expected. She looked up from her reading, "How was dinner, dear?"

Benton continued to read the paper.

"It was not earth shaking, mother," Paige answered.

"The earth, doesn't need to shake. Look at your mother and me," Benton said, from behind his newspaper.

"Oh Benton! What a thing to say to your daughter," Connie admonished.

"Mother! Dad! I have something important to tell you," Paige interrupted.

"What is it, dear?" Connie asked.

Benton looked over his newspaper.

"Dad! What happened to your eye?" Paige exclaimed as she ran to her father, and gently touched the bruise on his face.

Benton was a softy where his daughter was concerned.

She cradled his face in her soft hands kissing the discolored cheek then she cuddled him in her arms. "What happened, Daddy?" she repeated softly.

"A scalawag got in a lucky punch. I don't want to talk about it. What did you want to tell us?" he asked.

She stood proud and smiling, looking from one to the other, "I've leased an apartment," Paige announced.

Benton threw his newspaper down, shouting, "What? No! I won't have it!"

"But Paige, what will our friends say? A young woman with your upbringing going off to live alone?" Connie asked staring at her daughter as a frown creased her brow.

Paige started to answer.

Benton barked, "Connie don't prattle. The answer is no! It's unheard of in this family!"

Paige raised her voice, "Mom! Dad! This is the year two thousand and one. I've made my decision, "I'm moving and I hope you'll try and live with my judgment. Can't you be just a little happy for me?' she asked. "You've instilled good values in me beside I lived on my own in Switzerland a continent away."

"We know that dear but that was a sheltered environment, and with your upbringing … " Connie finished weakly.

"The lease is signed and all the arrangements are made Mother," Paige said. Her voice was soft but inflexible.

"Don't talk to your mother in that tone of voice!' Benton exclaimed, pacing the floor red faced. Stopping to catch his breath then shook his finger at Paige, "A year two thousand one woman, hooey! You've always been an obstinate and unruly child!"

"Oh daddy, you love it besides I prefer to think of it as a mind of my own," as she hugged him, "You'll see me so often you won't know I've moved," Paige said laying her head on his shoulder. "I love you and Mother very much so let me try this."

She went to her mother and held her hand kissing it," Mom, it's time for me to find my place in life."

"Ashley should have married you last year after that very expensive engagement party," Benton said gruffly.

"Benton! That wasn't the time!" Connie said.

"What kind of place is this you've leased? How will you live? Just tell me that?" Benton demanded.

"I have a penthouse in Old Town. You forget I'm a writer, and there's my inheritance. June is on her own and doing well," Paige answered.

"What kind of living is that?" Benton asked. "June is no example, she's always been a little strange! Did she put this nonsense in your head?"

"No Daddy it's my idea, besides my book was well received in Europe it's in the second printing, and the possibilities are good for the United States. There were discussions of a movie deal, and a large sum of money," Paige said.

"Chump change, that's what it's called," Benton grumbled.

Paige looked at them, then said, "I'll manage very well Daddy, don't worry. I've planned this carefully. I was taught by the best you know,"

"Who?' he asked.

"You Daddy," Paige answered.

Benson's chest puffed out as he tried to hide a smile.

"But Dear … all by yourself!" Connie said, still concerned

Paige went over to first one and then the other, embracing them. "Don't worry so. Have I ever let you down? You'll be so proud of me, you'll have goose bumps," she said.

"Huummuph," Benton said, clearing his throat.

Page laughed and hugged her father extra tight, "Daddy, don't start your bear act with me, you old sweetheart. I'll be just fine, really. You and mother didn't raise a foolish child. Anyway you're always here for me if I need you, right?" Paige asked as she walked out of the room.

Connie stared anxiously after her.

Benton, trying to hide his pride in his daughter picked up the newspaper and settled noisily back in his chair with a broad grin on his face.

CHAPTER 2

◆

On Friday, June Sawyer, Paige's childhood friend had lunch in a picturesque café overlooking the Marina. There was a panoramic view of the bay and beyond to the lighthouse on Starks Island with yachts and sailboats on the horizon.

"I told my parents about the apartment," Paige said.

"What did they say?"

"Mother is worried about what her friends will think as usual," Paige answered.

"What about your dad?" June asked.

"You know him, he was his old self, grumpy, trying to control my every move." Paige answered.

"Does he realize you're a lot like him? You both are inflexible. The only difference is you're not grouchy," June giggled. "I would have liked to have been a fly on the wall to see your father's face."

"He turned purple as he always does," Paige said, and they had a good laugh at Benton's expense.

June spread her arms, saying, "Look at me I didn't turn out badly. I've had my apartment for two years. Now I'm vice president of one of my father's companies, and if I must say I'm quite good at my job. Sales are up dramatically."

"Yes, but your love life is a mess," Paige said pointedly.

"Don't be silly, I've been in love at least twice this month," June giggled and looked at Paige, asking. "You're going to Brooke's party, right?"

"I'm not sure," Paige said. "I'll discuss it with Ashley."

"Oh him. Mr. a place for everything and everything in its pulace," June said contemptuously

"Oh you, of course with him, we're in a serious relationship you know," Paige responded.

'I'll give you dimes to donuts that marriage will never happen. I've been looking around for someone with a lot more life than, Ashley Boregard Smith." June said, emphasizing her statement with the forefinger and middle finger on both hands.

"We respect each other, but I wish he would do something illogical at times," Paige said wistfully. "I'll change that when we're married."

"Paige if you're married it's too late. Phooey on him, you go to the party. I'm going, but with who I'm not sure."

"That's with whom madam vice president," Paige corrected.

"So I flunked grammar. This is a hypothetical, would Ashley call you at two in the morning?" June asked.

"No, of course not perish the thought!'

"And, if he met you in a crowded lobby of a posh hotel would he kiss you passionately in front of the people there?"

"No!" Paige said horrified.

"Then my next question is not a debatable point." June said.

"What's the point?"

"While in this posh hotel, would he drag you off to a room with champagne then screw your brains out?"

"You're so bad. No!" Paige said giggling.

"I think he's very dumb, and I'm certain Ashley won't like Brooke's party," June said.

"Why not? Ashley is really quite friendly." Paige answered.

"He reminds me of someone with a very bad hemorrhoid pucker," June said giggling.

"He's not that disagreeable you nut," Paige admonished, but was forced to laugh.

"Let's talk about something more meaningful, like what we're wearing,"

June said changing the subject.

"We know the kind of parties Brooke is noted for." Paige said.

"Yeah tight dresses showing lots of skin," June said grinning.

"And nobody has more skin than Brooke."

"I think I'll wear the gown from Megan's, what do you think?" June asked.

"I love it, it does a lot for your figure," Paige said.

"Change of subject. Did you hear about Anthony Jordan?" June asked.

"No, what about him?" Paige responded. "Our family doesn't talk about the Jordan's you know that."

"Sure I know about the stupid feud, but it can't hurt to talk for God's sake," June said as she paused. "Well, anyway he was having one of his tantrums, yelling at the judge on the tennis court then he threw his racket and left the court very angry after a game. He raced away in his car, had a blow out then collided with a cement road divider. Tony has a shattered pelvis and a broken leg," June said.

"That's too bad, how is he, I assume he lost the match?"

"Yep, he lost. The newscaster said he left the hospital last week. However, the game of tennis is over for him." June answered.

"I thought he was a promising player," Paige said.

"Won ninety percent of his matches, used some kind of self actualization system." June said.

"Greek to me." Paige said.

"By the way what was that nutty feud about between your families?" June asked.

"I haven't a clue. It happened so long ago. I was just a child. My father always turns red in the face when he reads in the Money Maker Daily about the Jordan's." Paige said.

"You probably will never know, if your parents remember themselves. Things like that usually take on a life of its own then really get out of hand as the years pass," June looked at her watch, "Gotta go, I have a meeting."

Paige signaled the waiter, "Check please." They paid and tipped the waiter, then walked out of the café chatting.

In William Jordan's office he was with his assistant Bernard Ericson. A yes man in tailored suits who tried to emulate his boss.

"Ericson I want a listing of stock holders in Cray ton Industries." William said.

"How soon do you need them, sir?' Ericson asked.

"The end of the week," William said.

"I'll get on it right away, sir." Ericson said.

"While you're checking, make a note of the Prendergast holdings," The assistant scribbled on his pad. William continued, "We'll need as many major stock holders as possible."

"Will that be all, sir?" Ericson asked as he stopped writing and looked up from his pad.

"William deliberated momentarily, then said, "If I think of anything else I'll call you."

"Anytime, sir," Ericson responded as he packed his briefcase then left the office.

William turned in his chair to face the window, staring into space chuckling. His office was bordered on two sides by windows that allowed the watcher to see one hundred and eighty degrees in both directions. The decor was comfortably opulent, affluence without being ostentatious. His mirth was not because of the view. William was apparently seeing something beyond his lofty perch, when the intercom buzzed.

"Yes Kim?' he answered.

"Your son is here, sir," Kim said,

"Send him in!" William exclaimed.

Anthony came in on crutches. He was tall, in his mid-twenties, ruggedly handsome, athletic and clean cut.

William went around his desk to arrange the ottoman for Tony to elevate his leg.

"That's some cast, does it hurt much?" he said, marveling at the length of the cumbersome cast.

When Tony was settled William sat across from his son with a concerned smile on his face.

"Not much pain, the problem is carrying the cast around and these damn crutches," Tony said.

"Is it true, you can't play anymore?" his father asked.

"Yes, the orthopedic specialist doesn't think so. My pelvis was crushed, causing damage to the sciatic nerve. Along with the compound fractures of the fibula, it's too near the knee to stand the stress of tennis."

"That's too bad."

"It's healing nicely, but intense sports play is over, and my gait shouldn't be effected," Tony answered.

"I don't want to go through anything like that again. Your being hurt and almost killed had your mother and me terribly worried."

Tony chuckled, saying; "It had my attention, too. A near death experience gives one a whole new perspective on life."

"I'm sure. What are your plans now?" William asked, and touched his son's knee lightly.

"The worry I put you and mother through for a moment of temper was unforgivable. I'm sorry about that dad," Tony said.

"Well what are parents for?" William asked.

"Not that kind of anxiety," Tony hesitated, then said, "When I was in the hospital I had ample time to think, and make plans," he was silent again for several seconds, then continued, "I had this idea and want to run it by you."

"Okay, shoot," his father said, and crossed his legs draping an arm on the edge of his desk to listen.

"I've been looking at old factories and I found one suitable to use as a school for young hopeful tennis players. I plan to train promising athlete's, sponsor tournaments and manufacture tennis equipment, and other paraphernalia," Tony said enthusiastically.

"Can you make money that way?" William asked.

"Yes, it's a very lucrative business, I know because my equipment cost me a fortune," Tony said.

"You should know," his father said.

"There's a young man I've been keeping my eyes on him, Omar Stevenson. He's a hell of a tennis player, dad. Omar recently won the Harvey Cabot Intercollegiate Tennis Tournament while still a sophomore in State College. I have it all worked out, and with the money I've made from the tennis tours and my inheritance, I can swing this project. The structures are sound, and won't need much renovation. Later I may take on one or two partners. What do you think?"

"You've done all right so far, and you have a good head on those broad shoulders. But no more temper tantrums." William said.

"That's over." Tony responded.

"Where is this factory?" William asked.

"Edgewood. It was a bottling company. Art Deco built in the round. It has good grounds, flat surfaces, lots of space for the courts, and pools, actually there are other buildings on the property, it's a steal. One I can use for living quarters and another as a dormitory for the trainee's."

William said, "I read about a young black man who is playing exceptionally well. Is he the one you have in mind?"

"Yes, that's him, Omar Stevenson. I saw films of him while I was in the hospital; He has that rare natural athletic ability. I haven't seen anyone like him in ages. He has one extraordinary dimension I've never seen, he's ambidextrous. But I read about it."

"This is good?" his father asked.

"It's not usual in a tennis player, and it happens on rare occasions. It's a plus in his and my favor." Tony answered.

"Do you mind if I take a look at this building?" William asked.

"I was hoping you would ask. When?" Tony replied.

"I'm the boss so how about now?" William said smiling.

"Now! Great! Let's get this show on the road. You'll like this set up," Tony said struggling to stand adjusting his crutches.

"It sounds like a sound idea. I'm with you one hundred percent. If you need help, mom and I are here. My companies will sponsor the purses." William stopped before opening the door, saying, "But I think we'll take my car today you don't drive," then he stood aside as he opened the door.

"I came in a cab letting someone else do the driving for a while," Tony said. They both chuckled as they left the office.

"Kim, have my driver bring the car to the south entrance. I'll be back in time for my four o'clock appointment." William instructed.

William walked beside Tony, "Ambidextrous? And that's a good feature?"

Tony nodded.

"I seem to remember a young man some years ago. Is he the same one that succeeded in All City, and later took over the regional games while in grade school?"

Tony nodded again.

"The same Omar involved in that civil rights thing at Alta Vista Tennis Club?"

"Yes, he's the same man, and I agree with his stand at Alta Vista by the way. That was a scandalous situation turning the people away with police in riot gear." Tony answered.

"We should have done something long ago," William agreed.

"Omar, has won over eighty percent of the tournaments while a sophomore in State College. I would like to take him over if he'll turn pro." Tony said.

"Can you do that?" William asked skeptically.

"I can try, his coach died recently, and he might not want to quit school in the sophomore year, so why not? I will try anyway. He's my last difficulty to over-come." Tony said.

"How much capital for Omar to start?" his father asked when they stepped into the elevator.

"Five hundred thousand at least, but the guy is worth every penny and more," Tony said, "I will make him an offer he can't reject. He'll make a mint of money in no time and I'll come out of it smelling like a rose."

"You make it sound easy," his father said.

"It won't be that easy. It'll be hard work grooming him for the nationals, the U, S. open and finally the crème de la crème, Wimbledon."

They walked across the sidewalk just as the limousine glided to a stop at the curb.

During the same twenty-year interval an African American boy was raised. In another world and a more deprived area on the other side of town.

In the late nineteen seventies two police officers were involved in a shootout with fleeing bank robbers.

Officer Omar Stevenson yelled into his microphone, "Officer needs help! My partner is down!" bullets tore into his cover as shards of glass sprayed the area.

Sirens are heard in the background.

Stevenson was hit, mortally wounded as he emptied his police special into one robber.

In the mean time his wife was in City hospital delivery room as her husband lay dying.

Mildred Stevenson gave birth to a screaming baby boy. The infant was brought for her to see. Her eyes devoured her new born sons face. She said weakly to her sister, "Evelyn, we'll name him after his daddy, he is Omar Stevenson Jr. Edie, I am so tired, and I won't be here to see my husband. Tell him I love him and to raise Omar as we had planned." Mildred whispered, as the nurse took the sleeping baby back to the nursery.

Evelyn answered softly, "Everything will be as you want it Mildred, you can tell Omar yourself." She held her sister's hand.

"No Edie, this is the last thing I can do for my husband, a fine baby boy," Mildred said weakly.

Evelyn held her sisters hand as Mildred breathed her last.

Evelyn and her husband Jefferson Stands stood looking at the baby Omar through the viewing window in the hospital.

She said, "I couldn't tell her that Omar was killed."

"I know, dear," Jefferson said.

"We have a son now, the child we've never had. Is that okay with you?" Evelyn asked.

"Yes, I can take him to the park with me, and teach him about tennis. I'll be able to show him a lot of things," he answered.

"Sports again, I'm glad I'll be there to teach him the basics of life. Go to church, tell him about his parents." Evelyn answered.

"School teachers, can always find a way to ruin a guy's day," Jefferson said.

"But now we have to make final arrangements for Omar and my sister." Evelyn said, as she took one last look at the baby.

The funeral took place on a dreary day with a large presence of fellow policemen. Thirty-nine motorcycle officers led the funeral procession to the Grant Christopher Memorial Cemetery in columns of three. Officer Omar Stevenson's coffin was draped with the flag of the United States.

Evelyn and her husband Jefferson Stands sat with the infant Omar at the graveside, beneath a canopy.

The minister said, "We lay these souls to rest, in the name of the Father, The Son, and the Holy Spirit. Amen.

Officer Omar Stevenson was given a twenty-one gun salute, and fellow officers solemnly folded the flag and the Chief of police, somberly presented it to Evelyn for baby Omar.

Evelyn and Jefferson Stands were childless, and took the baby Omar to raise, the same as their parents had brought them up. He was a patient man who tended the equipment, and was overseer of the grounds keepers at the county park. He followed every tennis game and tournament played by Arthur Ashe and others. Compiling clippings, tennis memorabilia and stories from Althea Gibson and very good tennis players throughout the years.

Omar at two dressed up as best he could like the tennis players he had seen at the park. His picture album was created over those years along with the tennis volume. He followed his uncle Jefferson around as a toddler dragging an old tennis racket, sucking a pacifier. Before Omar was four he was taking swings at the ball and connecting most of the time.   Jefferson spent long hours teaching his adopted son everything he knew about the game.

"Omar I want you to hold the racket with a firm grip and concentrate on where the ball will be in a mille-second."

"Like this, Uncle Jefferson?" Omar asked, as he held the racket for his uncle to see. " Is this a Mille-second?"

"That's good son." Jefferson answered, as he adjusted the child's grip. "The purpose of the game in my judgment is to score, and win."

"Yes, Uncle Jefferson." Omar said.

He held Omar's shoulder's, saying, "And you never imitate a known player. God gave you a brain so you have to create your own style, whatever is comfortable for you within the bounds of correctness," Jefferson said and tapped the child's forehead, "That's where you play the game of tennis in your brain, your mind."

"I have a good mind, huh uncle Jefferson?" Omar asked.

"Yes son. Your Aunt Evelyn will help you develop your mind. I'm here to help you explore your game. You have to let it evolve without rushing."

Omar asked childlike."What's evolve?"

"Let it happen don't rush. Get to know how you feel, work on your timing use what works for you. Develop your own stance and meet the ball on your own terms, with power. Even if the ball goes high or wide, hit it and knock it out of the park if necessary then control your swing." Jefferson said.

"I can do that uncle Jefferson."

"Yes you can son, and I'm here to see that you learn everything you can," he answered.

At the Brookside Tennis Pavilion the pro and security guards put Jefferson and Omar off the court's, saying, "This is the last time I'm telling you to stay off the courts. The next time I'll call the police! Can't you understand you people are not wanted here! Take your junky rackets and stay away from here!"

"This is a free country we have rights, I fought for the United States!" Jefferson said.

"Not at this Pavilion, I don't care who you fought for." Then to the guards, "See that they get off the grounds."

The guards walked behind them making snide remarks, saying, "Is your brain to thick to understand this is the sport for white people?"

Omar looked up at his Uncle Jefferson, who took his hand as they walked through the gate.

One guard, yelled, "Remember now, no jungle bunnies allowed!"

"Uncle Jefferson, why don't they like us? We didn't break anything," Omar asked.

"That is the way some people have to show their importance, they lord their authority over others." Jefferson answered. Then said, "Come on we have work to do at the park."

"Why did we go there, Uncle Jefferson?"

"I wanted you to see other tennis courts beside the one's at the park, Brookside has grass and clay courts, you're used to playing mostly on concrete."

"Why?" Omar asked.

"You needed to see the grounds. One day you'll be playing on them and you will win. We can take a little stupidity from a couple of jerks." He answered.

When Omar was eight he and his uncle had been thrown off all white's only tennis courts of Los Coronado, California. It was because of his steadfastness, and his exceptional ability that the tennis pro at the park took a serious interest in his game.

He was entered in park tournaments and won eight out of ten games.

At ten the park pro and various clubs in Los Coronado had taken an active interest in Omar, and marveled at the boy's ability. He was tall and strong for his age and held junior ratings in the National Tennis Association. Omar enjoyed one on one competition, and read voraciously. His grades were excellent through school.

Aunt Evelyn said, "You're good at tennis but you also have to be good with your mind when it comes to your studies."

As he played the game, he won and lost in the park. In high school his ability and resolve developed. Omar grew into a brilliant player, a true athlete. He could hold his own in Junior American football as a quarterback, in track and field he was no piker, he sprinted with good timing and leaped hurdles. His baseball game was good. But the sport was too slow for him. Basketball and soccer he never tried.

Omar needed the one on one competition and always came back to the game he loved most, tennis. He ate and slept the game, playing it better than well, winning throughout his short college career.

Devon Sharp a reporter discovered him at an early age and followed Omar religiously, with hometown boy does well type stories.

Aunt Evelyn retired when Omar was fifteen. She and Uncle Jefferson along with coach Winters from the park attended every game he played.

Uncle Jefferson died suddenly in his sleep before the county regional.

Omar won the county and regional competitions handily, he said softly, as he played, "For you Uncle Jefferson."

He lost in the State Finals.

Omar complained, "I shouldn't have lost that match Aunt Evelyn," and slumped in a chair down in the dumps.

Aunt Evelyn said, "You have to be thankful for the gift God has given you. You lost because you were getting a little too cocky. And God had to take you down a peg or two." His aunt was there to teach him the finer things in life along with family values.

"Did he have to do it during the State finals, why now? I wanted to win that for uncle Jefferson." Omar said.

"Your uncle knows honey. This was just the maker's way to let you remember where your gift came from. This isn't the end child you still have a lot to learn, you did learn something, right?"

"Yes, I did learn something don't try too hard."

"So take your time and master your sport." Aunt Evelyn said.

Omar the child had grown into a handsome African American man with clear intelligent brown eyes. A strong body with long strides, and reach and the ingenious mental capacity to execute his play. All that was lacking was experience and a chance to play and grow into his chosen sport. His mode of dress of faded laborer's bib overalls and a red, blue or yellow farmer's bandana folded as a sweatband. He had made inroads into the game at the parks, and high school winning championships.

He participated in sit-ins at the Alta Vista Country Club where the policy was no minority was allowed membership or to play. Group's of young people marched with placards, pasted leaflet and did sit in's to draw attention to the clubs policy.

Chanting "Alta Vista Country Club is bias don't support a racist organization!"

Police arrived and had to carry the students away.

Headlines blared, "Omar Stevenson a rising young African American tennis player carried away by police. He joined the sit ins at Alta Vista and highlighted the racist rules of the club. The white's only rule was the basis for the U. S. Tennis Association to re-evaluate the policies of all the clubs across the country, or lose their standing.

Omar became the focal point in the civil rights struggle in the city. Now it was being played out in a tough match on the tennis court. He came from being down one set to win.

A reporter, asked, "Was your win today in retaliation for the past policies of the club?"

"I never thought the social significance was due to my efforts. There were a number of people who had an interest in the clubs polices, we happened to agree, " He answered. Omar at twenty-one, had won the U. S. Amateur Tennis championship at Alta Vista Country Club.

Construction was nearing completion on A. J. Enterprises. Tony was returning from the site late one evening when he drove by the county park, and stopped to watch Omar hit balls off the board in the public park. He walked over using his cane and sat on the bleacher.

Omar's sweaty body was like a well-oiled machine, proportioned, good reach, great balance and exceptional ability. He finished his workout and ran two quick laps around the track, then came over and plopped down on the bench beside Tony.

"What brings you to this side of town?' Omar asked., patting his face dry, then draped the towel around his neck.

"You did. You're a high profile player," Tony said.

"Do tell." Omar answered smiling.

"Yes, I've watched you play throughout your sophomore year," Tony answered.

Omar nodded.

"And then, I saw more film of you while I was in the hospital. You are mind boggling; I couldn't believe what I saw. So I came to see the man who almost single handedly won the intercollegiate Tennis Tournament for State."

"And?" Omar asked.

"It's all true, the reports didn't go far enough." Tony said.

"Thanks." Omar replied.

"I'm opening a school and arranging my first tournaments. First I want to persuade you to turn pro and second, I want you to play for A.J. Enterprises, for at least three years," Tony said.

"Sounds tempting, but Aunt Evelyn won't hear of my leaving school. I'd lose my scholarship. You'll have to take it by her, and that won't be easy." Omar replied, then added, "I read about your accident. Tough break."

"You know about me?" to Tonys surprise.

"The bad boy of the circuits? Of course I know about you. My uncle has you in his scrap book," Omar said laughing.

"Is that right? Could I see his album sometime?" Tony asked.

"He's dead now but Uncle Jefferson would be happy for you to see it, he liked you thought you had spunk." Omar said.

"Today?" Tony asked.

"Huh? Today, now?" Omar questioned.

"Yes. May I see the scrapbook today, and talk to your Aunt Evelyn?" he answered.

"If you want, Aunt Evelyn won't mind. I live four blocks from here, can you make it on your leg?" Omar asked looking pointedly at Toney's cane.

"I really don't need this cane much anymore. I'll drive us there." Tony saw the expression on Omar's face, added quickly, "It's safe I promise, no speeding. I've learned my lesson." They walked toward his car, "Where did you learn to play like that?" Tony asked.

"Uncle Jefferson mostly, the county park system and I had the park pro, then other coaches," Omar explained.

In Omar's neat, modest home his Aunt sat in the living room reading when the front door opened, "Omar is that you?' she called.

"Yep it's me and I have company, are you decent?" Omar asked playfully.

"Don't trifle with me of course I'm decent. Bring this person in here," the young men came into her view, "Hello. Don't I know you?" she asked, gazing at Tony over her granny glasses.

"Aunt Evelyn this is Anthony 'Tony' Jordan."

"Yes I remember, you're in Jefferson's scrapbook! Come in! Sit down! Omar get the man a cool drink. "Milk, lemonade or orange juice, of course water, those are the choices," she said agreeably.

"Lemonade please," Tony said, chuckling as Omar left the room. "I want to talk with you, too," he said.

"Me, really? What about?" Evelyn said.

"I'd like to persuade Omar to turn pro this year."

Aunt Evelyn looked at him again over her glasses, saying, "Omar will lose his scholarship he can't do that, honey."

"Don't speak too soon, let me tell you what I can do," Tony said quickly, stopping to look at her. "Stay with me on this."

Evelyn nodded and laid her book aside.

"My company will deposit five hundred thousand dollars in an account for Omar up front. I would like to groom him for the U.S. Open and later the Australian and so on to Wimbledon the cream of the tennis world."

Evelyn started to speak again but he held up his hand to stop her, saying, "Don't answer now think about it. I'll go so far as to deposit the money he would lose in scholarships, tax free. And later if he wants to go back to the University, he can. In addition when my company is up and growing Omar will be allotted a block of stocks, to be decided later."

"You have the confidence of the young," Evelyn said.

"Omar has the athletic ability, and I want to make him a wealthy man," Tony said.

Evelyn sat in silence considering his offer.

Omar came into the room with a pitcher of lemonade and tumblers. He served his guest and Aunt Evelyn, saying, "We serve people once in this house then you make yourself at home and serve yourself, no exceptions. I'll get the album," and went to a cabinet across the room and returned to sit beside Tony, he said, "This is it. Needless to say Uncle's album has clippings of Anthony 'Tony' Jordan the bad boy of the circuits."

Tony looked through the album.

Evelyn asked, "Omar do you know what Tony wants you to do?"

"Yep he told me," he answered offhandedly.

"What did you say?"

"It sounds good, but the final decision is up to you," Omar answered.

"Don't decide now, wait and discuss it. Think it over for a few days then get back to me, say in a week," Tony said. "I also came to see this album," as he turned another page.

That's a plan," Omar said.

They laughed and talked while inspecting the photo album of clippings until late into the evening, and drank two pitchers of lemonade.

Tony left reluctantly with the promise to return soon. Omar and his aunt agreed to discuss his offer.

Ten days had passed, Aunt Evelyn was persuaded.

"It's a lot of money, but your education is important, too." Evelyn argued.

"I'll make you a promise, I'll go back and finish my education during the breaks. It's my promise to you on my honor." He said.

"It's not the money is it?" she asked.

"Auntie, it's money I can use to start a clinic in my own neighborhood to teach the kids at the county club to train and learn to play tennis, think about it." Omar answered.

"Your Uncle Jefferson always wanted to do that for the neighborhood children." Evelyn said.

"I can do that in his memory and get my education along with it," Omar said.

"My folks always said education first but this is a new generation." She looked at him, and said, "On your honor you can do this, but I'll be watching and cheering."

Omar picked her up in a bear hug and swung her around.

"Omar, put me down!" she said laughing.

The business arrangements and financial agreements were completed. The Attorney's had left the boardroom. "We have a short time before the tournaments begin, and there's a great deal of hard work ahead." Tony told Aunt Evelyn.

"He's up to hard work," she said.

"Omar, I want you to stay at the school for the next few weeks. The coaches can start grooming you for professional play." Tony said.

"The real world, Auntie dear," Omar said.

"I'll help you pack," she replied laughing as they stood to leave.

"Don't bring too much, just sweats, shorts, things like that," Tony said as they walked to the elevator. "I'll expect you tonight. You need to be rested for our morning routines. Shall I pick you up?"

"I'll be here no later than nine," Omar answered. As they stepped into the elevator, "See you then, chief,' he said with a half salute.

The doors to the elevator closed.

Chapter 3

♦

The night of Brooke's party the guest's drove along a tree lined Suburban Boulevard with neatly trimmed hedges. Toney's low slung sports car rolled smoothly along passing palatial homes that snuggled comfortably behind fenced and gated seclusion along the mountain road.

He was escorting Janet Claude the movie starlet. A shallow woman who fussed with her makeup and hair in the compact mirror, "I don't know why you're so upset it's only business." She said.

"I mean you're seeing a lot of this Miles Glenn maybe too much," Tony answered in frustration.

"That's for publicity, you know that," Janet said, rubbing imaginary lipstick off her front teeth then licked her full pouting lips.

"Some publicity," he said disgruntled.

"Miles will be here tonight so don't make a scene," she said, making a final inspection of her hair before she put the compact away.

"You invited him?" he demanded.

"I told my manager, he called the hostess and she invited Miles," she corrected.

Tony swerved into the stone driveway at Brooke's and turned the automobile over to the valet then escorted Janet to the front door.

The house was built in relationship with the mountain and a stream that flowed through the trees. Stone and nature held its own in a living and dramatic way. Brooke's dead husband had his architect design his mountain home on

Snake Road with his own subtle touches.

Double falls served two purposes, the first being dramatic falling water to please the viewer from the gardens.

The second was taller and visible at a distance with sheets of cascading water, the sound of falling water was soothing from the patio.

Mirror ponds and a lane for walks were added at the higher elevation to heighten the effect of nature and man together.

The house seemed planted there to confront its surroundings as though it couldn't exist in any other setting except here. It rose majestically out of a concrete water table rooted in the landscape, symbolizing life and energy, a self-portrait of the man who built it.

Tony escorted Janet across the cobblestone space to the door, and was met by Clive, Brooke's houseman who directed them through the home to the patio. The inside of the house was opulent and, breathtaking.

Janet stopped in awe as she looked all around at her surrounding décor then on to the patio where small clusters of people chatted.

Music was played in the background as they followed Clive outside. The party was in full swing as gyrating couples danced around the pool. A live band played in a niche designed for that purpose.

Janet looked eagerly around, saying, "There's my manager. I'll just say hello," she left before Tony could say anything, he watched her progress as she wiggled her way around the dancers.

Beside her manager was Miles Glenn along with a photographer that eagerly took pictures of the two cinema personalities.

Brooke was thirty-ish and in addition to her incredible dimensions, a voluptuous woman, lovely tonight in a low cut black gown. She moved from one group to another, smiling and chatting for a few seconds and then on to the next assemblage. Brooke was never the shy type and accepted her role as a widow philosophically especially when voicing her opinion, she employed the frontal attack at all times.

Brooke spied Tony as he ambled across the patio, "Tony! You've finally arrived! You good looking devil, and so handsome in mid night blue." Brooke said, as she hugged him making kissing sounds on either side of his face.

"This is quite a party, what's the occasion?" he asked.

"It's in memory of my late husband rest his soul. Spencer liked parties so I have one for him, sometime twice a year," She smiled prettily hugging Toney's arm, "Must there always be a special occasion for a party?"

"I suppose not," Tony said and laughed as he turned to the bar, "Scotch on the rocks, please."

"Spencer always liked my little gatherings," she said. in a husky seductive voice.

"You're looking gorgeous tonight, as usual," Tony said.

"This is our little mutual admiration society, you delectable devil." Brooke said.

"He took his drink turning to her, saying, "Careful now, you'll turn my head."

"If only I could," she breathed, "but there's somebody else I want you to meet."

"You know I'm in a situation as we speak," he sipped his drink looking around, "So is this lovely lady here tonight?" Tony asked.

"She is here somewhere, I haven't seen her in the last few minutes," Brooke said, looking over the guests searching for her choice for him. The one she was looking for was on the other side of the patio, "There she is now, come I'll introduce you."

Toney's attention was elsewhere as he set his glass down quickly, saying, "There's Janet dancing with that actor, Miles Glenn. I'll talk to you later," he said, and kissed Brooke on the cheek then hurried toward the dancing couple.

"Tony, that relationship won't last!" Brooke said, to his back as he crossed the dance floor. she continued softly, "You really should meet my friend."

Tony tapped Glenn on the shoulder, the actor turned Janet over to him, "We have to talk," Tony said to Janet.

Just then Gregory Banks who was slightly drunk, with his arms around two pretty women, said loudly, "Tony, how's the tennis racket," he snickered, "Get it? Tennis racket."

"I get it Greg. Tennis is great and getting better every day." He answered as he led Janet to a secluded corner of the patio.

Gregory hugged the girls and led them to the bar, saying, "Well, what'll it be my lovely's? I'm having scotch rocks" then leaned on the bar and looked at the bartender with expectancy as they decided what to order.

On the dance floor, Brooke was swaying to the music with Eric Prendergast surrounded by other couples.

Eric was the good-looking son of a friend of the Cavanaugh's and a college acquaintance of Toney's. "My tooth brush is packed for travel," Brooke said coyly.

"On really?' Eric said and smiled with one eyebrow raised.

"I could curl up beside you when the party is over," she said softly.

"I'm tempted to take you up on that," he answered.

"My kind of a guy," she said moving closer.

"The feeling is mutual," he said, as he cradled her in his arms.

"That's what I like about you Eric so agreeable," she said.

At that moment Eric was slapped on the back with such force he almost fell into the shrubbery.

It was Kenneth Bellingham a big Texan, and college friend of Eric and Toney's. Kenneth's expensive suits never seem to fit quite right, and he seldom talked below a shout.

"This is some party ma'am. You know how to shake a leg, and what pretty legs, too," he said, followed by a loud, "Yee-haw!"

"I'm glad you are enjoying yourself," Brooke said, a little taken aback momentarily, then she grinned broadly.

"Brooke this is Kenneth Bellingham he went to the university with Tony and I," Eric said.

"Where did you find her?" Kenneth asked in a loud lascivious whisper.

Before Eric could answer Kenneth slapped him on the back again in the same spot as before," I'm proud of you fell a! She's built like a brick out house, solid, good in the withers. She has stamina, yes, my, my," he said grinning, shaking his head with pleasure as he lifted Brooke and whirled her around bodily.

"I'm sorry Brooke," Eric said massaging his shoulder.

"I'm not, this is a straight shooting' fell a, let the man talk," she said,

"Ken doesn't look at a pretty woman, he ogles them boldly," Eric said apologetic.

"Yes sir-ree this is some woman! Are you from Texas ma'am?" Kenneth asked as he kept up his appraisal, when he lifted her, and whirled her around, yelling again, "Yee-haw!"

Just then someone fell in the pool. Others saw how much fun that must have been and followed suit by jumping into the water in their evening clothes, squealing, splashing and laughing.

In another corner of the garden Janet Claude slapped Toney's face, shouting loudly for the reporters. "I wouldn't marry you if you were the last man in the United States!"

"I'll drive you home … " Tony started to say.

"Don't bother! I'll take a cab!" she retaliated loudly posturing for the press and pictures, then stamped away into the interior of the house.

Tony went to the bar.

Ashley, Paige and her friends left at that time.

The party raged into the night with music, dancing and gales of laughter.

Morning dawned sunny and bright at Toney's roof top poolside. The building had been converted to a luxury apartment along with the tennis center. He and Gregory were unshaven sprawled on lounge chairs, dark glasses shaded their blood shot eyes from the sun. Ice packs deadened the pain. No one noticed the panty hose hanging from the umbrella, glasses strewn around. Gregory wore one sock half on one foot.

"Never again will alcohol cross my lips," Tony mumbled.

"That goes double for me. I'm definitely swearing off all vices and turning over a new leaf," Gregory said and rolled on his back gingerly placing his head on the pillow.

"How about some tomato juice?" Tony asked.

"That might be good," Gregory said looking over his glasses.

"Who's going to get it?"

"You suggested it you get it, I'm not well." Gregory said.

"Let me rest a minute," Tony said, flopping back on his chair.

"Did you see Samantha?" Gregory asked.

"I couldn't miss, I'm swearing off women," Tony said, "At this moment seriously thinking of becoming a Monk, why don't you join me?"

"They grow grapes, make wine, and pray a lot." Gregory said.

"I'm not sure right now, Gregory" Tony said, "Who cares anyway?"

"That's a good business, we'll be rich."

"We are rich," Tony retorted.

There was a loud whirring noise from the kitchen, starting and stopping.

"What the hell was that!' Gregory asked raising his ice pack.

"Probably your imagination I can't hear anything over this buzzing in my head," Tony said, massaging his temple.

"I tell you I heard an un-Godly noise," Both winced when the noise started again. "Oh my God. Oh my God there it goes again!' Gregory said.

"What sadist would be working this morning?" Tony asked as he struggled to sit up and grope his way toward the kitchen, saying repeatedly, "This was a bad idea, bad idea, very bad idea." His grumbling was lost to Gregory who couldn't be bothered.

Omar was in the kitchen, dressed in crisp white tennis shorts making tomato cocktails. He stopped to stare when Tony came in disheveled. "Wow Anthony you look like something the cat dragged in yesterday."

"Yeah right," as he sat at the counter and took his dark glasses off, asking, "Did you practice your backhand?"

"Of course I did," Omar said, as he looked at Tony, "Whoa! Where did you get those eye balls, man?"

"I'm not really sure they don't seem like mine, and who cares anyway?"

"What did you guys do last night?" Omar asked.

"Things got a little fuzzy, all mixed up after midnight," Tony answered, holding his head.

Omar turned back to the tomato cocktails, saying, "Who was over last night? Maggie was upset because the place was a mess."

"Some of the guys came over after Brooke's party. We had old fashions, then some boiler makers and depth chargers, to name a few." Tony stopped, then asked, "You say Maggie was upset?"

"Let put it another way. Maggie was pissed when she said this place was littered. What did you guys do to get on her bad side?"

"My night wasn't clear, I told you that already. I'll call her," he yelled, "Maggie!" holding his head.

"What?" a voice yelled back.

"Maggie dear, come in here please." Tony answered.

"I'm busy Anthony!" the voice said.

"I need your expertise."

Moments later a voluptuous black woman dressed to go out came through the door, "I repeat, what do you want Tony?" Maggie looked at Tony and started to laugh. "If you have a bad head that's your problem, my dear. I told you last night, you would be sorry."

Tony looked at Omar and shrugged, "She told me last night. I don't remember any of it, after mid-night is a blur."

"I did warn you. Now look at you, a pathetic wreck of yourself, and all because of that Janet Claude," Maggie said adjusting her hat. "I'm going out, and don't mess up this place. I'm not cleaning it again, not today. I have shopping to do you want something special?" Maggie asked.

Tony shook his head, and she left pulling on her gloves.

"That Maggie, salt of the earth," Tony said. "Are those cocktails for us? Old Greg's in bad shape."

"No sooner said than done," Omar said pouring two goblets and shoving them across the counter. "There you go."

Tony replaced his dark glasses, slowly starting in the direction of the patio, carrying the drinks.

"How about a hail to the chief, Tony?" Omar said raising his glass.

"I don't have the strength, " he answered going toward the door.

Omar followed reading the newspaper; they joined Gregory on adjacent lounges. He read aloud, "Janet Claude international film star danced the night away with Miles Glenn at Brook Topplinger's party Saturday. This reporter asks this burning question, Is Anthony Jordan history?"

As they drank a part of their cocktails.

"They are what is known as an item now." Tony answered massaging his jaw. "She emphasized my historical value last night," he added reaching for his ice pack and tenderly placed it on his forehead.

"Brooke said she has the right woman for you Tony," Greg said.

"I need a woman like the plague. I'm off women. Well hell, life is in doubt at the moment." He said settling back to recuperate.

"How about this Clive character, what's with him?" Greg asked.

"Gay as the proverbial blade, now I need my rest." Tony said Omar   tossed the panty hose aside then settled back to read the paper and sipped his tomato cocktail the other two fell asleep in the midst of the of their messy surroundings.

CHAPTER 4

◆

Paige came into the Cavanaugh front hall as the telephone started to ring, Saturday afternoon. She walked quickly to answer, saying, "Hello."

"Paige? Ashley here."

"Ashley, are you home?"

"Yes. Is dinner still on for tonight?"

"Is eight good for you?" she asked,

"Perfect," he paused. "Sweetheart, wear the green gown tonight," he instructed.

She frowned and hesitated momentarily, "For you dear, yes."

"Splendid, I'll see you at eight."

She said softly as she placed the receiver down, "Never mind that I never really cared for that particular gown. I have the right everything! There must be more to my life, a little more excitement, anything!" as she slung her purse over her shoulder and ran upstairs.

The focal point of dinner at Ashley's club was the site that complemented the restaurant on an exclusive plot of real estate near the golf club. The building rose among the carefully manicured lawns, terraces and urns, as part of the exterior arrangement.

The foliage that trailed from the upper cantilevered façade softened the Roman brick.

Inside, the walls were elaborately paneled in an atmosphere of quiet refinement. The first floor contained the Bistro Bar, billiard rooms, quiet spaces and other areas designed for men only.

On the second floor are extended open expanses on that level, interrupted only by the decorative fireplaces separating the dining room sections. Windows opened onto terraces, lengthening the dining area out to overlook the natural setting, with a magnificent view of the city in the distance.

The third floor housed suites of rooms with hot tubs and spas with balconies and a spectacular sight of the surroundings.

This Historical Landmark remains among the most celebrated structures in the city of Los Coronado.

After dinner Ashley and Paige joined Tom and Ellen Clemens party, friends of Ashley's and an older crowd than Paige.

"That last act, …" Tom was saying, when the couple joined them.

"Ashley! Paige!" Ellen interrupted, "I'm happy you could come! You know everybody don't you Ashley?" then she said, "Paige dear, you're lovely tonight as always. Green is your color."

"Thanks Ellen," Paige replied.

"It's been a while, Tom, Carl, ladies," Ashley said, shaking hands with the men and bowing to the women.

Tom resumed the conversation from before the interruption, "Now, back to Tyler Johns play. I didn't like the last act, it didn't fit."

"On Tom, it made the whole play worthwhile," Ellen said, grasping his arm smiling affectionately.

"I saw it in New York, and I agree with Ellen. It was a good melodrama, and the ending was perfect." Paige said.

Tony Jordan stopped by the group.

Ellen exclaimed, "Anthony! I think you know everybody except Ashley and Paige Cavanaugh."

Tom made the introduction, "This is Ashley Boregard-Smith, Paige is his fiancée. Folks meet Anthony Jordan retired tennis player."

Tony kissed Paige's hand, "The pleasure is mine," he said to her, then shook Ashley's hand, "Is that, Smith Industries?"

"Why yes it is, how do you know about me?"

"Sit Anthony, don't stand on ceremony. " Ellen said.

"I know of your vast holdings through my father," Tony said as he sat across from Paige.

After the exchange Ashley turned back to the previous conversation.

"Now, back to that stinker of a play. It isn't good work it's trash. I know some of the acting is good, but acceptable actors can't save a clinker like that. It'll probably run only a few days or a week at the most," he said with emphasis.

The vivacious young woman across from him captured Toney's attention, and he didn't miss the change of expression on Paige's face following Ashley's summary of the play. He looked at her lingeringly several seconds, then said, "Ms. Cavanaugh…"

"Paige, please." She answered.

"May I assist you? More coffee?" he asked.

She nodded.

Ellen protested in the background, "You men! You don't appreciate the real beauty of this piece of work."

"My sentiments precisely," Paige said.

"I know I'm right," Ellen argued, "Thank you Paige dear," turning to Tom

Paige withdrew into herself blocking out dinner noises around them as she watched Tom, Ellen Ashley and the others. She looked at their faces amidst the composed quiet hum of voices from the surrounding tables; all were older and stodgy. In those few moments she felt separated from their hum drum lives as a sense of freedom stole over her. Ashley was engrossed in the argument and was not aware of the change in her demeanor.

Tony observed her puzzling metamorphoses during his scrutiny of Paige. Even though he didn't know what had caused the change, he felt drawn to her immediately

He said, "Ashley, may I have this dance with Paige?"

"Yes, yes of course," was Ashley's detached answer, then turned back to some other topic of discussion.

Tony guided Paige to the dance floor. Their closeness sent a jolt through them both. It was electric as they stopped momentarily to gaze into one another's eyes. The irresistible urge to hold her was stronger than anything Tony had ever felt, an impulse that was overwhelming.

He held her comfortably close as they danced the length of the floor oblivious to the other dancers; her head barely reached his chin as their bodies formed a fluid unit. His nostrils flared as the subtle fragrance of her perfume stole into his senses.

Page was acutely aware of every point of contact between them as her soft yielding body followed his every turn.

When the strains of the music faded he reluctantly released her.

His voice was husky, as he said softly, "Thanks for the dance, I want to see you again, have dinner with me."

She was taken aback by his appeal.

"When can I see you?" he repeated, lightly touching her shoulders.

Paige looked toward her table, Ashley was still engrossed in conversation. A frown creased her brow as she faced Tony, "Call me tomorrow, my apartment is in Seton Towers west, I'm in the book."

Tony drew a deep breath and escorted her to the dinner group. He regained his composure on the way. "Thanks for the dance, Paige," he said softly.

"I enjoyed it," she replied smiling. Her smile transformed her face from lovely to radiant.

Tony drank in her fresh beauty as he kissed her fingers.

He said, "Ellen I'm sorry to leave so soon but I have an important matter that needs my attention."

"Tony, must you go?" Ellen asked petulantly.

"Yes Ellen I must, it's an important matter," he answered.

"I saw your first tournament," Ellen said as she gushed over him, "You have a great find in that young man. Oh what, is, his name?"

"His name is Omar Stevenson, he's doing well. Tennis is his game. We're lucky to have him playing for A.J. Enterprises. Gotta go Ellen," Tony said, looking at his watch.

"Tell your mother I'll call her soon," Ellen said.

"I will," Tony answered, and turned after a last look at Paige, then walked quickly away.

Ellen stared at his retreating back, saying, "My goodness, he is in a hurry."

Paige felt a letdown, left in the depressing presence of Ashley and his stuffy friends. Mentally she asks herself if this is all her life is meant to be after her marriage. Long dull evenings being pushed into the background? The bewilderment showed on her expressive face.

Ashley noticed her quietness, and was mystified momentarily. He didn't understand her expression as he leaned closer, saying, "Mother would like you to come for dinner, can you make it Friday?" he asked and squeezed her hand, smiling.

"Let me call you," Paige answered.

In the conference room at A.J. Enterprises, "Let's start with Omar's statistic's. Kirk, we'll discuss all his strengths and weaknesses."

Kirk spread his folder open, and said "Physically the man is in tip top shape, for the shape he's in, and that's great. He doesn't like aerobics and is a fugitive when it comes to vegetables. Other than that his weight is within normal guidelines. Muscles are solid. The doctor said he's a-one. His first tournament dazzled the press, he's a crowd pleaser. In his short career he has a following of young people. They're wearing faded bib work overalls and bandanas."

Tony turned to Avery, and asked, "What's your view?"

"He has one unorthodox capability. An edge so to speak. It's seldom if ever seen in a tennis player," Avery answered."

"We know about that." Kirk said.

"Omar rarely if ever serves into the sun because of being ambidextrous," Avery said. "He hits exceptionally well with both hands, the left might need some work but not much."

"I saw that during the games, and didn't mention it. Actually the change took me by surprise," Kirk said.

"He doesn't use the left all the time; it's compensation when he needs that little extra edge. I became aware of it one afternoon when the sun was bright," Avery answered.

"How is he on the courts?" Tony asked.

"He's use to asphalt, and does his best work there. Needs some work on clay, and grass slows him down a bit."

"Put that on things to work on. How are his legs?" Tony said, pausing momentarily. "I appreciate the fact he has excellent court presence as a matter of fact he's magnificent."

"Omar's that alright, he's not cocky. The strength in his legs is fine. He's a natural athlete, everything he does works for him. Hell, the man knows his tennis for one so young. He must have had a hell of a teacher. He knows things I've long forgotten and have to look up." Kirk said.

"He had an excellent teacher. You should see his uncles scrapbook, it has my statistic in it, too." Tony answered.

"Another thing he hates is to lose, the kid plays every match as if it's his last. His shoulder strength and arms reach is uncanny. His ball speed is one hundred and twenty plus miles per hour after his sizzling laser like service. Omar is young and getting better. He's rated number sixty-eight in the nation now. The kid's awesome," Avery said.

"I'll be around to see him develop," Tony said. "Omar will have his chance against one of the best, and soon." He shuffled through the pages of a note pad, "Now bring me up to date on the others, especially the new woman trainee, Najha Blander."

They opened their folders.

In the Cavanaugh dining room the next day, the family was having dinner with June, and Paige, who said, "Mother, Ellen said she would call you next week."

"Thank you dear. When did you see Ellen?" Connie asked.

"At dinner last night." Then Paige asked, offhandedly, "Mother, did we ever know the Jordan family?"

Benton stopped dropping a fork full of food a short distance from his mouth, he said gruffly; "We did, but not anymore."

Connie tried to stop her daughter's next question by shaking her head.

"I never met them while growing up. Why?" Paige asked.

Benton twisted his glass around on the table cloth, and answered tersely, "William Jordan is a crook and we don't do business with double dealing tricksters!" he said and gulped his wine.

"Calm down Benton," Connie said soothingly. "Why do you ask Paige?"

"I met Anthony Jordan last night," she answered and sipped her wine.

Benton choked and wiped his mouth as his face turned red.

"Are you all right dear?" Connie asked solicitously.

"Of course, 'I'm all right dear'," Benton said mimicking his wife. Then turning to Paige, he said emphatically, "Paige I don't want you to have anything to do with this Anthony Jordan, person."

"But why? He seems harmless enough. He is certainly a good dancer," she answered.

June looked from one to the other growing uncomfortable.

"The father is a charlatan! The whole damn family's integrity is open to discussion! From the father on down to the son" Benton was livid.

"Dad! I won't be doing business with him," Paige answered with surprise. "Beside I've never seen you so upset about anyone I meet. It was only a dance and he was very charming, no horns or tail," Paige reasoned.

"Now dear, don't get yourself so agitated," Connie said trying to placate Benton.

He grew redder in the face if that were possible, and bellowed.

"Connie I'm not getting agitated! I'm already furious!" He stopped talking to catch his breath. "Nobody in that family can touch my daughter, and get away with it!"

"Paige I think I had better go," June said and started to rise from the table.

"See what you've done Benton? You've frightened June," Connie said reprovingly.

"I have done no such thing, June knows me by now," Benton said, peevishly as he fought to control himself.

"Stay June dear his bark is worse than his bite," Connie's tone was conciliatory.

Paige laid her fork down to watch her father,' "Daddy why are you so agitated, this can't be good for your blood pressure. Your anger has to go deeper than my dancing with Tony Jordan. Why can't you give me a reason?" she asked.

He cleared his throat loudly.

"Later dear," Connie said quietly to her daughter. As she rang for the maid. When the servant came, she instructed, "Georgia Mae we'll have coffee in the drawing room, please."

"Yes, Mrs. Cavanaugh. Will that be all, ma'am?" Georgia replied.

"Yes, thank you," Connie said and the maid left the room

Later in the evening in Connie's dressing room, "Paige and her mother sat comfortably facing each other.

"How are you and Ashley getting along dear?" Connie asked.

"There are times I think I'm not ready for marriage," Paige answered, then said, "Mother are you going to tell me what happened between our family and the Jordan's?"

"Yes dear right now." She paused momentarily, "We all went through college together. Patricia later married William, and then Benton and I were married. You were born in July, and Anthony was borne the next April."

"He's younger than me?" Paige said.

"By a few months. At the time our families seemed destined to be lifelong friends, but your father and William went into business together after the University then there was that awful falling out." She paused momentarily.

"That was a bad idea," Paige said.

"I missed Pat, and I threw myself into community work, we just sort of grew apart after that. The years went by so fast it's twenty plus years already," she concluded softly

"I never knew that." Paige said. " But mother Mrs. Jordan was your friend like June and me. I couldn't let June grow away from me."

"Your father would have gone into a rage if I had continued to see Pat and she understood, we were both in the same situation."

"It wasn't fair." Paige said.

"I know dear, this all happened when you and Tony were toddlers," Connie replied.

"Daddy hates him after all these years?" Paige asked.

"Let me finish dear, after one business dealing went wrong your father lost money and you know how he hates to lose especially in money matters," Connie said.

"But they were friends didn't they both lose money?" Paige asked.

"Yes of course they both lost. Your father blamed William and you know your father, pigheaded. Neither one would apologize for the harsh words," Connie said.

"Did Dad go broke?" Paige asked.

"No. Nowhere near it. Oh he's generous sometimes to a fault. He said William was a crook and at times I think he is trying to convince himself of that very thing. You see, they loved each other like brothers. I think that love is still there even after all these years. Back then if you saw one the other would soon show up. But Benton doesn't like to fail. He has this thing about money and business just like his father before him," Connie spoke the last few words facetiously.

"Yes, I remember," Paige responded, as they settled back for a laugh at Benton's expense.

CHAPTER 5

♦

Tony sat on the deck near the pool, watching Maggie dust, "Maggie I met a very foxy woman recently," he said adjusting the strings in a tennis racket.

Maggie turned and looked at him, saying dryly, "Not another Janet Claude?"

"She is extraordinary. Not a mindless body jiggling show off, but a woman I think I could grow to seriously care about," he answered.

Maggie enumerated on her fingers, saying, "Now let me see where have I heard that before? There was the one in Barbados; I'll call her what's her name. Then there was that one in New York, let us not forget New Orleans, and the list goes on up to and including Janet the wiggler."

"This one is different she make you feel like settling in a vine covered cottage. I'm thinking of connubiality."

"They were all different, if my memory hasn't failed me," Maggie said, "But connubiality, is startling."

"There are two minor difficulties," he said.

"I knew there would be a catch! What are the minor problems?" Maggie asked.

"She is Benton Cavanaugh's daughter," Tony said offhandedly.

"Uh ooh," Maggie said, with one hand to her lips. Then she started to grin, and her chuckle turned into a belly laugh.

Tony stared at her in surprise, with his hands raised, "What?" he asked.

Maggie controlled herself, saying, "I haven't seen that child in a long time, but I like her already," she stared him in the face, "So what is the other problem, is she married or missing an eye?"

"She is engaged," he said.

Maggie took a deep breath and blew it out, "I thought you were going to say she was damaged, engaged is nothing," Maggie frowned, and said, "Engaged to who?"

"The word is to whom," he corrected.

"Works both ways for me, you know what I mean." She said.

"Engaged to Ashley Boregard-Smith," he replied.

"That pompous ass! He was born old! His parents were old when they had him, what is he now, thirty five or forty?"

"Thirty something." He said.

"What is he doing with a young girl like her? I say save her, go for it."

Tony jumped up laughing and kisses her cheek, "Maggie you are the light of my life. By golly I think I will! Great advice!" he said as he danced her around the room.

Maggie was out of breath when he stopped, she said. "That's enough of that. I say why not, you're aggressive in business and at tennis. Tony I would suggest you get off the dime and do it, rescue that child," she said.

Outside the Jordan Building a reporter held a mike in front of William's face, "How do you respond to the Cavanaugh statement that you are no businessman?" he asked.

"I would answer by saying, to me business is special, it is pure competition. There are those who can stand against all odds, and then there are those who snivel and complain. What can I say?" William answered.

"Was that a personal evaluation?" the newsman asked.

"Nothing personal it's a known fact, there are men who transact business and there are those who can't. I know some who can't," was William's urbane answer.

"There was a number of small take over during the last twenty years, and seemingly the need to win at all costs," another newsman asked.

"I have said it all along a victory no matter how small is just as sweet. It is a compilation of sound negotiations and the intelligence to strike a deal based on valid business principles," William said.

"It has been known to the press over the years that Mr. Cavanaugh says you are a charlatan and a litter bug when it comes to handling your affairs," the questioner replied.

"He does have a way with words, but I need to point out that a tale told by a simpleton signifies nothing. Besides I never argue with muckrakers, and mental cripples. Now if you will excuse me I have an important appointment to keep," William answered, and left the reporters standing in his wake calling out questions.

"And there you have it, ladies and gentlemen. Cutting answers from one of the adversaries in this feud over the last two decades," the newscaster said.

The Smith estate stood behind vine covered walls with pillars that resembled sentries at the ends of the circular driveway. Majestic oaks graced the property.

The sedate beauty of the home started with the impressive entry through magnificent double doors. In the hall one saw the handcrafted staircase. Hardwood floors gleamed in the light from the chandeliers, in the sunken living room with its precisely placed Persian rugs. The broad front windows were floor to ceiling and offer an imposing view of the mountains in the distance. The room housed a marble fireplace as the room flowed toward the spacious formal dining area with its panoramic view of the city lights. An ideal place to enjoy dinner with friends. French doors open on three sides to a terrace for entertainment that overlooked the elaborate pool house and spa two terraces below near the dock In addition there were naturally grown trees and other plantings bordering lush lawns, and bridal paths that led to the stables and pasture.

The estate had Old World trappings a sought after haven in the age of the millennium.

Ashley's father made his first fortune in pig iron, coke, decorative iron works and other similar undertakings. The Smith's were patrons of the arts, trustee's of the Robanian Library and other interests and businesses.

The cream of Los Coronado society was at the Smyth's. The super rich in the personage of the Ogilvy's, the Hale's and the Oppenheimers's. Dignified pillars of Los Coronado. Laughter was held to a minimum as quiet music played in the background under the subdued conversation.

The aperitif before dinner was served elegantly as the guests nibbled the morsels of tiny sandwiches.

The meal was an affair of excellently prepared foods befitting any majestic occasion, noted on the opulent table setting. The appropriately dressed, domestic employee's catered the meal, befitting royalty.

All courses were served in composed tranquility as Paige listened to the restrained dolcide tones of conversation.

Mrs. Smith said, "My husband was always interested in politics. We are Republicans you know, and we need our man in the White House."

"I agree, we need up standing young men like Ashley to take over the reins of their fathers," Mrs. Oppenheimer said.

"Oh and speaking of reins, I have meant to ask you Paige dear, do you ride?" Mrs. Hale asked.

"Not well I'm afraid," Paige answered.

"Ashley rides as if he were born to the saddle, he'll get you started on the right foot, dear." Mrs. Smith said.

Ashley leaned over and squeezed Paige's hands and smiled.

"I must mention the art exhibit, a pet project of mine is opening in two weeks, we need all your participation," Sheila Ogilvy said and looked back and forth at the guests along the table.

"The opera guild is opening soon there are so many things for us to do this year, between appointments, the horse show, and I can't miss my trip to Europe this year." Mrs. Hale said.

Paige listened to the other mundane chitchat.

"Paige dear, you're so quiet tonight." Mrs. Smith said.

"I am just absorbing the atmosphere of this wonderful home," She answered.

Mrs. Smith turned back to the guests to her left.

Paige shuddered and looked around at all the other guests and thought this is dinner at the Ashley's.

Finally there was dancing to dispassionate music and after dinner drinks, with more conversations.

Paige danced with Ashley.

"After we're married this will all belong to us," he said, as he smiled down at Paige.

"Ashley, I don't know what to say," Paige said, without enthusiasm.

"Don't think about it now just savor the idea, ours forever," Ashley announced proudly as they waltzed around the floor.

"They make such a handsome couple, I remember him as a child such a manly little tyke it's difficult to believe he's all grown up. Now look at our little Ashley engaged to be married," Mrs. Oppenheim said as she turned her head and followed as the couple dance around the floor.

"It's not easy to believe he's thirty five, the time has flown by," Mrs. Smith said as they watched Ashley and Paige.

Soon the affair was over and the guests started to leave at the appropriate time, in the midst of fond farewells and chauffeur driven limousine.

This was dinner at the Smyth's, Paige shuddered again at the thought of her life in this atmosphere.

The next Monday Paige was at her desk working on her script when the telephone rang. She finished a sentence before answering absentmindedly, "Hello."

"Is this Paige Cavanaugh?"

"Yes." She answered.

"This is Tony Jordan."

"Hello Tony Jordan," she said cheerfully.

"Will you have lunch with me today?" he asked.

"I don't know if I should be speaking to you, our families are feuding you know," Paige answered lightly.

"That is old news. I remember the servants whispering about it over the years but that has nothing for us to be concerned about," Tony said.

"Apparently it does, my father read me the riot act for mentioning your name," she said and smiled.

"You mentioned my name?" he asked pleased.

"Yes, I was curious about our families, and the feud." Paige said.

"I repeat, how about lunch?" Tony replied.

"I can't. I'm seeing Ashley off after lunch," she said.

"That's even better, I'll pick you up for dinner at eight," he said, placing the receiver down before she could answer.

"We'll see about that Mr. Anthony Jordan," she said as she looked at the humming instrument and smiled.

Tony arrived promptly at eight, dressed impeccably for his date. He spoke to the concierge in reception, saying, "Mr. Jordan to see Ms. Cavanaugh."

"Ms. Cavanaugh left this note for you, sir," the concierge said passing an envelope over the counter.

"Thank you," Tony replied.

The legend of the note as he read. "I am sorry but I have a previous engagement and can't dine with you tonight. If you had stayed on the line a moment longer your wasted time could have been avoided," signed Paige Cavanaugh.

He folded the note and left the foyer chuckling.

In William Jordan's office Ericson, sat across the desk from him, saying, "I have the information you requested, sir. Sorry I'm late."

"Splendid! This is a timely enough," William said enthusiastically reaching across for the thick folder. Glancing through the report briefly. "Excellent!" He repeated. "Superb work," closing the folder then turned to Ericson. "You have done it again. There will be a generous bonus for this," he said tapping the report.

"When do we start, sir?" Ericson asked.

"I'll keep this under wraps until just the right time. Wait for my cue," William said chuckling happily.

"Yes sir, will that be all, sir?" Ericson responded as he closed his briefcase preparing to leave.

"I think that will be all for now, Ericson. This is outstanding!' William opened the folder again, delighted. He called out before his assistant could close the door, saying, "Ericson? I have been looking at the local football team. Let it be known quietly in our usual places that I'm interested, and thanks again." William said and leaned back in his chair laughing.

It was a perfect Monday for anything, but work.

A gentle breeze was fresh and cool as the sun rose like an orange ball over the horizon. No trace of the smog that usually hung likes a shroud over the valley after days of constant rain.

There was an exuberance in June's mood as she sipped her first cup of coffee of the day. She had a commanding view of the skyline. In the distance the bridge spanning the bay and beyond. The glassy smooth surface of the Pacific Ocean was glazed orange by the sun.

A neighbor waved to her from his balcony before turning and going inside June saluted him with her cup as she turned and, going into her penthouse. She walked through the specially appointed apartment with its opulent décor, plush white carpet and a scattering of ultra modern furniture.

June went to the kitchen through the sunken living room, rinsed her cup and put it on the drain.

She was an energetic young woman dressed for the business day; her suit clung to every curve of her slender figure. June crossed the living room again stopping to give herself the once over in the mirrored wall. A final touch to her hair and a closer look at her perfectly applied makeup, turning first one way and then another to survey her body in the mirror.

June looked at her watch and exclaimed, "Oh damn! I'm late again!" she grabbed her purse and hurried out the entry hall door.

In the elevator she watched the numbers as the car slipped smoothly down the elevator shaft. She rushed across the spacious lobby and out the front as the doorman opened the door.

"Good morning Ms. Sawyer," the doorman said.

"Hi Alfred, Sam have my car ready?" she asked.

"Here it is now," he answered.

The small convertible was driven into place at the curb. Sam, the valet climbed out and held the door open for her.

"Thanks, Sam," June said and jumped into the driver's seat.

"No problem Ms. Sawyer," Sam answered, as he closed the door then stepped back.

"Have a nice day," June said waving as the little car leapt away from the curb and roared away down the drive. Slowing momentarily then sweeping into traffic. She pressed the accelerator to the floor as she weaned in and out of traffic.

As she neared her place of business June glanced into the rearview mirror to see the flashing lights of a police car. Reluctantly she pulled over and looked anxiously at her watch.

The officer climbed out of the patrol car and ambled slowly to the driver's side of the convertible.

He looked with appreciation over the racy little car as he approached; asking, "Did you know you were doing fifty five in a thirty five mile zone?" his voice was deep with mellow tones.

June gazed up at the impeccably groomed policeman, with wide-eyed innocence. And, she was acutely aware of his becoming mustache and warm brown eyes.

"Oh officer I'm so sorry," she answered. "Was I really driving that fast?" she asked, reading his nametag, "Officer Jack-obey?"

"That's, Jacoby, and yes, you were really doing fifty five. You should keep it below Mach 2," the officer said. He observed the way her clothes clung to her slender body. And the short skirt revealed her shapely legs.

He asked, "May I see your driver's license please?"

June rummaged around her bag then handed him the license.

"And your registration," he requested.

She leaned over and removed the document from the glove compartment and gave it to him.

"Do you work near here?" Officer Jacoby asked.

"The sawyer Building," June answered.

"Very close by, and you are June Sawyer?" he said, as he read her papers more closely.

"Yes, that's right Officer Jacoby, and I'm so late for a meeting," she said pleading.

"Ms. Sawyer, I shouldn't do this but I will overlook your speeding this time with a warning," he said, holding her papers lightly in his hands.

Surprise and happiness transformed her face from delightful to radiant.

He cautioned, "Remember, this is a warning. Next time you're caught speeding you will be ticketed and fined."

"I'll be careful in the future you won't catch me speeding again," June answered prettily.

"Your license and registration," he said as he returned her papers.

"Officer Jacoby, are you married?"

"No, I'm not."

"Do you go to cocktail parties?" June inquired.

"Yes, I do. Why?" He asked.

"You are invited this Saturday to a party as my guest," She answered and gave him her card. "Call me at that number, I'll tell you where and when."

"I'll call this evening," he said as he read the card.

"See you there," she replied, then drove away pushing the speed limit.

He stood in her wake then read the card in his hand again and thumped it once chuckling before going back to the patrol car.

Later that morning in June's office she dialed a number.

The telephone rang beside Paige's bed, she let it ring several times before answering. Then lifted the receiver, saying sleepily, "Hello, this had better be good."

"Paige, this is June!"

"I repeat, this had better be damn good," Paige answered.

"Why are you in bed so late? Did Ashley get horny in the night and come over?" June asked, facetiously.

"I have a deadline remember. I was up until past dawn finishing the screenplay," Paige answered.

"You're such a smartly pants. Guess what?"

"Come on June, no twenty questions at this hour."

June took a deep breath, before answering playfully, "A good-looking policeman stopped me this morning for speeding!"

"I know, you're in love again," Paige retorted.

"Practically, he's got it going on girl friend," June said giggling.

"You're a nut," Paige said affectionately.

"We must have a cocktail party Saturday!" June said.

"Why?" Paige asked as she turned over in bed.

"I've invited him to one, of course."

"Make it a party for two," Paige said.

"Good idea. I thought of that but I couldn't do that!" June exclaimed, "That would be a little too obvious."

"Ashley may have something planned for Saturday," Paige replied.

"Good for him, he's a stuffed shirt anyway," June said, and paused momentarily. "I am desperate, you're my best friend ever. Ashley can come, you bring him, he'll impress some of my more snooty guests."

"I don't know, he was thinking about going out of town," Paige said doubtfully.

"Will he be gone long?" June asked. "And don't I wish."

"I can say yes, tentatively."

"Don't be a party pooper. I'll find a guy for you. Anyway forget Ashley. Please come, I need your support," June asked.

"I'll think about it." Paige said.

"If you promise to come, my day will have been made," June said.

"You go to work, and I'll think about coming to your spur of the moment party," they both giggled and placed the receivers down.

Paige turned over, stretched then pulled the covers up to her chin.

CHAPTER 6

◆

It was the last match of the Tennis Tournament,

The announcer said, "This has certainly been an exciting Competition, this, this, … this is the upset of the week, Guy!"

"You're right there, Jim. I would never have expected this kind of game. We knew Omar was explosive on asphalt courts, but this is beyond belief," Guy said, pausing to take a breath, "Jakes was ahead, on his way to winning, now this, upset!"

"Jakes is not having one of his glory days. This Stevenson kid will go out in a blaze of victory, today. Jakes is worn out and making too many mistakes."

After another badly executed volley, Guy said, "Jakes isn't playing to win with shots like that. Usually at this stage in the game he is on the attack."

There was a burst of energy on the court. Stevenson kept Jakes on the ragged edge of collapse. Taking the risk of putting Jakes back in the game with a smashing backhand. Omar took a four, two lead. The crowd was ecstatic as the players changed sides.

Another long volley, then Omar belted a smashing forehand. Jakes was unable to return the ball.

Jim said, "They have been playing two hours and fifty four minutes!" He paused to watch, then said; "Now they're going to the fifth and final set. Omar is looking for his first major professional victory, today."

"You know Tony Jordan is his manager," Guy said.

"Yes, he was a good man on the tennis circuits." Jim replied as activity rallied on the court.

"Jakes rallied! He found the strength somewhere. Another long round and it's game, six all!" Guy said.

"They have to go to a tie breaker, Stevenson's advantage." Jim said.

"Have you thought of the endorsements? The purse alone is a cool two hundred and fifty thousand dollar bundle!" Guy said.

"I agree, this young man has it made, if he can sustain this momentum," Jim said.

"Jakes is having a bad time of it, he's running on empty, you can see his sheer exhaustion, … down break point, something's gotta give," Guy said.

"How would you like it if an energetic Omar Stevenson was climbing up your back, and running you all over the court?" Jim asked.

'Have you noticed, Stevenson is ambidextrous, he hits well from both sides." Guy answered.

"I noticed the switched hitting but I didn't believe it, so I waited for you to mention it," Jim said.

Guy described the action, saying slowly, "The serve and volley. Stevenson takes a four, two, lead. The players break, I have a feeling Omar is just hitting his stride."

"This new comer can take this match with two more points! And I believe he'll pull it off!" Jim said.

"Jakes hit the last serve directly to Stevenson, not the way to win in my opinion. He's lost it," Guy answered.

"Stevenson moves comfortably from one foot to another, watching, well balanced." Jim continued to describe the action. "Jakes back he is against the proverbial wall. Stevenson is taking the fight to him. Thirty, fifteen, he runs down every serve and sends an explosive blast back to Jakes. God! Omar has a great lob! It's three love, final set with two breaks. Jakes appears totally wiped out. Stevenson never lets up! It's as if quitting was never an option for him."

Guy answered, "Jakes is showing unrelenting fatigue and Omar appears to be growing in momentum, chewing away at Jakes all the time, running him all over the court."

"Omar, after trailing two matches, now he is at three break point. He'll serve at five love when he comes back." Jim announced.

After a break in play Omar sat on the sideline mopping his face with a towel.

"He just gave the thumbs up sign to his Aunt Evelyn in the stands," Guy observed. "She's at all of his matches. Ah they are coming back to the court," as a burst of action began and continued for several what seemed like several drawn-out minutes.

"That was a long volley and Jakes could barely execute." Jim said.

"He appears in a lots pain," Guy said.

"After playing three hours and fifteen minutes. Who would have believed Omar Stevenson would come from behind to win this championship six, two!" Jim said.

Guy said, "This relatively new comer is the winner in hard fought sets. Jakes rating coming to the match was number twenty-five. He was beaten today by this neophyte. Ladies and gentlemen we hope you have enjoyed this unbelievable week of tournaments, sponsored by A.J. Enterprises."

Outside the arena the press surrounded the winner. "Omar! Now that you have the championship trophy, not to mention the lucrative purse, what is next or maybe I should say who is next for you?" the reporter asked.

"That hasn't been discussed yet. Those at A.J. Enterprises and I will decide that at a later date," Omar said.

"This was a stunning win for you. How did you feel out there today?" another reporter called out.

"I went out and played my best, that's what we came here to do our best, right?" Omar answered.

"You have a following," one reporter pointed out, "In the United States they are wearing bib overalls and bandanas just like yours. What is the significance of the way you dress after a match?"

"This apparel is my way of keeping my balance, and remembering where and how far I have come," Omar replied quietly, and looked around the assembled reporters momentarily, "Thanks, I have to go now. I don't want my muscles to stiffen up," as he pushed through the clamoring crowd of reporters and onlookers.

On Saturday at June's Cocktail party, she clung to the arm of the uncommonly good-looking Officer John Jacoby. They mingled as she introduced her newfound friend to her guests, chatting from one group to the other.

John fit in nicely, as he looked down at her with delight while she gazed up at him adoringly.

The caterers mingled with the guest as they served tiny sandwiches and glasses of wine, and a bar was set-up for stronger drinks. Lively music played in the background as a few couples danced on the balcony, and the wide landing of the living room. June and her friend John opened the door when the bell rang "Paige, Ashley do come in, this is John Jacoby. John this is my best friends Paige Cavanaugh and her fiancée Ashley Boregard-Smyth. Paige, you know everybody here introduce Ashley. My home is your home." As she led John to another group.

Paige's friends called to her and the chitchat was happily animated.

Ashley and Paige were occupied with two couples in a little niche across the room.

June giggled when she saw Ashley's discomfort, in these surroundings he was totally out of his element. His expensive suit was impeccable, which made him appear to have stepped right out of a tailor's shop.

Since Ashley's first drink he had looked at his watch. And as soon as it was socially acceptable he urged Paige to leave.

He said, "Paige, sweetheart, I have a matter that I must take care of very soon, would June understand if we left now?"

Paige approached June, and said, "June, Ashley has an urgent matter to take care of and we must leave. I am sorry, but we'll talk later."

June, with her arm around Paige and John in tow walked them to the door, "I am so sorry you have to go so soon that's a bummer, but as you said we'll talk later my dear friend, and thanks for coming." As she kissed Paige on the cheek then embraced Ashley and leaned back, saying, "Ashley you have never been to my home, but you have an open invitation to come again," she delighted in prolonging his unease.

"I will," he said the words as if they left a bitter taste in his mouth then made a hasty departure as he guided Paige to the elevator.

William sat behind his desk and dialed a number, when the telephone was answered at the other end.

"Ericson here."

'Ericson, William Jordan you can start the ball rolling tomorrow morning at nine o'clock sharp, I want every proxy possible."

"Yes, sir." He answered, pleased that his boss had called him personally at home.

"Come to my office on Monday to make your report," William instructed.

Ericson made his report, "Sir, we have gone far beyond our expectations, all we contemplated and more are here," he said.

"Splendid," William answered, and reached across for the folder then glanced through the pages, saying, "You have done your work well. I have one more thing to do now. It will shake that fat twerp's foundation. I will take care of that myself this evening. Your task is over and well done. No, I will say you have done an exceptional accomplishment. Excellent work!"

"Will that be all sir?" Ericson asked with pleasure.

"Yes, I couldn't have done a better job myself Ericson, there will be a bonus and a cruise for this admirable job."

Ericson smiled and closed his briefcase and left the room with a satisfied look on his face.

William continued to study the contents of the folder, his chuckle turned into laughter.

Benton was watching the Monday evening news report, the announcer said, "A coup de grace was achieved today in the business world. Jordan Enterprises has taken over Cray ton Industries a little known company, a holding of

Cavanaugh Industries. We will keep you updated as the news develops, more after this message."

Benton jumped out of his chair and rushed to the telephone and yanked the receiver off the hook. He jabbed furiously at the numbers on the pad and waited impatiently. He let the phone ring innumerable times when there no answer he slammed the receiver down.

He turned and bellowed, "Connie! Connie! Where is that woman when you need her?" Benton mumbled, "Connie! "As he moved toward the door to the hall.

They collided as she hurried into the room, "Benton, calm down! Why are you shouting?" Connie asked.

"That snake in the grass did it again!" he yelled.

"Who? What snake in the grass?" Connie asked.

"Who else! That, Jordan of course!" Benton shouted.

She put her arm around his shoulder and in a soothing voice, said, "Take a breath, and tell me what happened."

"He took over one of my companies behind my back Connie!"

"Was it a large company?"

"No, I acquired Cray ton several months ago, it's a small company I planned to check it when I have the time." Benton said.

"You can't take care of everything your general manager should take care of things for you." Connie said.

"It is my policy to see everything I acquire." he said.

"You can't continue with these tirades, no company is worth your health. Remember what Dr. Allan said, no more shouting. You could have a stroke," she paused momentarily then said in a reasoning tone of voice as she walked him across the room. "Benton dear, we made a vow 'til death do we part and I want you around a long time. I don't want to lose you, and think of our daughter. Paige would be devastated, you don't want that."

He tried to control himself while being guided across the room. She sat beside him on the couch and held his hand.

Connie had worked her magic and Benton was back in control and under her calming spell.

He clutched her hands in his. "No, I don't want that Connie." he said softly.

Paige was having coffee in June's office, overlooking the city.

"I hope Ashley wasn't too uncomfortable Saturday," June said.

"Are you really, sorry? He's not accustom to people of our set you know," Paige said.

"I am glad you said that," June replied.

"Ashley is not so bad, it does take a while adapting to us and our ways."

"Oh pooh, I'm glad you saw him amongst our people because he is not the right person for you to marry." June paused to take a breath, then changed the subject, "You will never guess who called me this morning?"

"Don't keep me in suspense. Who?"

"Officer John Jacoby," June answered smugly.

"That great looking guy at your spur of the moment cocktail party/" Paige asked.

June said, "One and the same," and grinned broadly.

"He was at your beck and call all evening. I thought you were a great looking couple. Is it getting serious?" Paige asked.

"You are absolutely right, we are in love." June said.

"June! You just met him, get real!"

"It was love at first sight," she answered and giggled.

"Oh come now let's get on the same page girlfriend," Paige chuckled, "It doesn't happen that way."

"This is as real as it gets. Paige, it's as though we have known each other all our lives. We have talked about everything into the wee hours. He whispers to me on the telephone, his voice so soft and deep it gives me goose bumps." June said.

"I don't want my friend hurt so take it slowly," Paige said.

"Me hurt, never," June said as she stirred her coffee, then smiled mysteriously, "You will be my bridesmaid."

"Now you're getting married?" Paige asked surprised.

"He doesn't know it yet," June said.

"John should be the first to know, you nut!" Paige said.

"He will in due time, but you are my lifelong friend therefore you are the first to know," June said and laughed uproariously.

Paige threw up her hands in surrender.

June asked, "Can we salute with coffee?" June asked.

"Who cares just do it. Saluda! To a long awaited marriage," Paige answered as they both laughed toasting each other with coffee.

In Brooke's home with a tea tray between them, she sat across from Tony, who said, "I have tried to get to know Paige Cavanaugh but this damn feud between our fathers is getting in the way, and there is her engagement to Ashley. I thought we had a dinner date, and I received a Dear John note. Of course that was my fault."

"Is that silly feud still on?" Brooke asked, throwing her hands up in annoyance.

"I am afraid it is alive and well," he answered.

Brooke said, "Nuts to that, you kids belong together."

"You and Maggie's feelings are the same, in your own unique ways," Tony said and smiled.

"Women of intelligence, how is Maggie?' Brooke asked.

"She is great, but back to the subject at hand," he said as he leaned forward with his elbows on his knees. Saying, "I have seen her around through the years then we met again and I danced with her. Oh man, but Ashley Smith her fiancée was there."

"Oh that pompous ass, he's all wrong for her," Brooke said and waved her hand in dismissal of Ashley, she paused momentarily, then her eyes lit up, "Paige plays tennis with June every Thursday afternoon at the club," then asked, "Do you still play?"

"Yes, just to keep in shape and I make my living that way in the business, then and now," he paused several seconds then continued, saying, "Brooke the night Paige and I danced everything felt right. I think she knew it too, I need to see her and talk with her without interruption."

"Well there you are it's not a problem. You go on Thursday I know exactly what to do," Brooke said excitedly.

"She might not talk to me," he said in doubt.

"You are a businessman who can arrange big deals and endorsements, and you are afraid to talk to a little woman?" Brooke challenged.

"Terrified is more like it," he answered.

"Tony I believe in this meeting so much, I am going to do something I have never done before," Brooke said.

"What is that?" he asked.

"Just be on the court at two, and you will know when you get here," she instructed.

Thursday afternoon Paige looked at her watch impatiently while taking practice back swings with her racket.

Handsome in tennis whites, Tony approached, and said, "Ms. Cavanaugh I saw you here I didn't know you played tennis?"

"My game is nothing special," as she looked at her watch again, "It seems I have been stood up by my best friend," Paige said, looking at him with suspicion, "Why are you here at this precise time?"

'Didn't you know my company has the up and coming tennis player of the century and we still play here," he answered.

"And that up and coming player, is?" she asked.

"Omar Stevenson, you have never heard of him!" He asked disbelieving

"As a matter of fact I have known Omar since he won all city. He blew them away in Monte Carlo recently and you manage him?" she asked.

"I persuaded him to turn pro after his sophomore year from state, and I might add he will be in the top ten in the next year. Of that I'm positive," he said emphatically.

"I am happy for Omar he has worked hard for it," she said, frowning at her watch then searching the nearest path. "That June, I will kill her."

"You, are impossible to reach by telephone," he said.

"I can't talk to you, our fathers are fighting!" she replied looking at him with indecision.

"What does a twenty-year-old plus feud have to do with us? We didn't start it, they did. So long ago they don't remember why," Tony said.

"Honor thy fathers," she responded jokingly.

"Fathers don't always know what is good for their children, and this is one of the times," Tony answered.

Paige stared at him doubtfully.

Tony asked, "May I see your racket?"

She gave it to him reluctantly, and watched while he took a few practice swings,

"How is your game?" he asked.

"Not that great," she answered.

He looked her over appraisingly her arms, sturdy legs and thighs, strong body, "You appear to be a strong person, this racket is a little light for you." He said.

"I was beginning to feel like a prized race horse, what would you suggest?" she asked less suspiciously,

"Here, hold mine and take a few swings with it. It is too heavy for you but you could use one just a shade lighter than that," Tony said.

Paige took a few practice swings, testing the balance. "Wow, there is a difference!" she said surprised. "Maybe there is hope for my back swing yet."

"He walked toward the other side of the net, saying, "Come on, show me your backhand.

She hesitated.

Tony looked back, and said, "Come on its only tennis. I need to see your backhand before I can help you."

She shrugged her shoulders and took her place on the court.

There was a montage of volleys, forehands, over head lobs and backhands; his last shot whizzed by out of her reach.

"Oh that was a great set even though you probably always win," she said out of breath.

Paige crossed to the bench on the sideline and patted her face and throat dry with a towel.

"You were giving me a run for my money, and your backhand showed improvement, but it will need more work," he said as he zipped the rackets in their covers.

Paige watched his hands, so sure.

"Now, how about dinner tonight?" he asked.

"Well I don't know," she said hesitantly."

"It's only dinner, maybe a little dancing and then straight home I promise, on my honor," he said raising his hands in supplication. His smile was charming as he mopped his brow with a towel.

"Since you put it that way, yes dinner at eight."

"The last time you said that, I received a Dear John note," he said and turned to her with a crooked smile.

"I was hoping you were a gentleman and wouldn't mention that. This time will be different, my word of honor," she said. "Could we go to the Sky Room at the Los Coronado Hotel?" her eyes convinced him.

"Okay we will go there," he said as they gathered their gear and left the courts. "When you lob the ball your arm should be in this position," he said as he demonstrated while they walked toward the hedges.

"Do you really think I could do that?" she asked as they went from view.

Paige was dressed in a simple black sheath slit to the knee, a light stole and small evening bag. Her hair was piled on her head in one of the more fashionable styles.

The revolving restaurant was atop the Los Coronado hotel as they looked at familiar sites over dinner. A band played in the background and a few couples finished with dinner danced.

"There's the Marina, and the bay beyond that and Hamilton Park, did your nanny ever take you there?" Paige asked.

"That's where I fell off the jungle-gym and fractured a finger. My mother was very upset and said I couldn't go on it again or so she thought. I had learned my lesson and the jungle-gym was my personal domain in the park after that, and mother never knew." Tony said.

"I have wanted to come to the Sky Room since June told me about it. This hotel was built while I was away in Switzerland," Paige said.

"I am glad you came and may I say you look spectacular tonight Ms. Cavanaugh." He said.

"The same goes for you, so handsome in mid-night blue," Paige returned.

"Let's get away from this mutual admiration society. Who is June?" Tony asked.

"Sawyer, my lifelong friend," Paige answered.

"You mean of the Sawyer Foundation?" he answered.

"The same, do you know them?"

"My father is on the board of the Foundation. I met June briefly at one of the fund raising functions several years ago." Tony said.

"I have never attended one, not my kind of evening." Paige said.

"My mother is the culprit she forced me to go." He paused momentarily, then asked, "What is your kind of evening out?"

"The mood changes sometime it's somber, dining and dancing, I like simple walks in the park. Then I can throw caution to the wind and have lunch in a far away city. At home you will find me at my typewriter working on my stories." Paige answered.

"When are you getting married?"

"The date has not been set," she answered.

Tony sensed a slight change in her demeanor when she answered.

"How long … " he started to say.

Paige said hurriedly, "Let us not get into our lives."

"Okay. Tell me about Switzerland why were you there?" Tony asked.

"I was in school, and when our family were together we traveled throughout Europe mostly and sometime in our country," Paige answered.

"Sounds wonderful." He said.

"What about you, where did you go to school and when did you start to play tennis?" she asked.

"My schooling was done mostly in the eastern United States, and my family traveled mostly on the other side of the world, Spain, Italy, Parts of Africa, England, France, and several other places." Tony answered.

"What about tennis?" she asked.

"I started to play at an early age, around eight." He said.

"You know I am older than you by at least eight months, mother told me," Paige said.

"I like older women or should I say you're robbing the cradle," Tony said.

Their laughter was open and honest.

Dinner was finished.

"Shall we dance?" Tony asked.

'Yes," she answered, and they threaded their way to the dance floor. The Latin rhythms of the music took over as they danced with abandon to the mambo and a really wild tango.

Toward the end of the evening they felt the warmth of each other's body as they danced slowly. Paige's head nestled beneath his chin as Tony held her comfortably close and she could feel his physical strength. His movements were sure as they moved around the dance floor.

Hours later outside Paige's apartment she unlocked the door and turned to face Tony, saying, "This has been a delightful evening. I haven't danced that much for a long time, it have had an amazing evening hanks to you."

She stopped speaking as they gazed into each other's eyes.

Tony gently took her face between his hands, "I have wanted to do this all evening," he said softly as he touched his lips to hers, his arms drew her close. Then with tongues tasting the warmth of desire stole over them sending their senses to heights unequaled in wanting.

Paige's arms crept up and around his neck as they became totally involved in the kiss. Their bodies molded together and they were acutely aware of every point of physical contact.

Tony released her reluctantly and both were visibly shaken, his forehead touched hers momentarily.

His voice was thick with emotion when, he whispered, "I'll call you."

"Yes, I have to go in-side," Paige said softly, and opened the door and hurried into her apartment.

Tony stood outside and started to knock then changed his mind. He leaned his forehead against the door jamb momentarily before he turned and walked quickly to the elevator.

Inside her apartment Paige leaned breathlessly against the wall. She could feel her heart thumping wildly because of the excitement of Toney's nearness. Paige hummed a tune as she danced across the living room and down the hall to her bedroom. She fell across the bed and lay there smiling, saying, "That was great! June would approve." She turned to the telephone and dialed.

The telephone rang beside June's bed; she rolled out of John's arms, and answered sleepily, "Hello?"

"June this is Paige. You can't guess what I have been doing this evening?"

"Now who is playing twenty questions and at two thirty in the morning." June said.

"I have been dining and dancing in the Sky Room at the Los Coronado hotel!" Paige said.

"With Ashley I suppose?"

"No, with Anthony Jordon. He can dance girlfriend." Paige said.

"You are kidding, or have you been drinking?" June said.

"And he kisses great, too." Paige said.

"You kissed him!" June said.

"It was mutual and earth shaking! Best kiss I've had in a long time."

"This could lead to bigger and better things in the future, everything is looking up, It worked for me, did you go up to the lovers suite."

Paige said, "No we just enjoyed ourselves." She paused momentarily, when June's last statement dawned on her, she squealed, "You and John?" she asked.

"As we speak," June answered.

"You little devil you didn't tell me, your best friend."

"Paige I tried, remember." June said.

"Yes, you did try."

"I am in bed. Now you go to bed unless there was more, I have a meeting in the morning. Bye." June said and giggled before placing the receiver down.

Chapter 7

♦

During the drive to his office William noticed Benton's limousine ahead.

He instructed his driver, "Pull up beside that car ahead." The two automobiles arrived at the stop sign together.

Benton's window was open.

William rolled his down and leaned out, saying, "Benton, any good business deals recently?" he said tauntingly.

Benton looked around surprised then in anger, he shouted, "You scoundrel! You won't get away with that low down skullduggery!"

"Careful Benton, remember your blood pressure, and how is your eye?"

Benton, red faced pushed his chest through the car window shaking his fist at William. He roared, "You lousy crook!"

The stoplight turned to green and William waved to Benton, saying to his driver. "Drive on," His laughter rang out as his automobile crossed the intersection.

Benton followed, and he was still leaning out the window shaking his fist in the air. When he sat back he grabbed the phone and dialed and waited, then said, "Paul, Benton Cavanaugh, I am picking you up in twenty minutes wait for me," he said, and slammed the receiver down.

He picked his associate up. And said, "Paul, I want that franchise, and the number one running back in the league the one we discussed last week. Money isn't a priority."

"Did you make your bid yet?" Paul asked.

"Indirectly." Benton replied.

"Why indirectly?" Paul asked.

"If it's known that I'm bidding for it the price automatically goes out of sight," Benton responded.

"I'll see what I can do," Paul said and stared at Benton with ambivalence and surprise.

"Get back to me as soon as you can, tonight if possible, but tomorrow at the latest," Benton directed.

"I'll do that. Have your driver drop me at Starks Restaurant."

Benton nodded to his chauffeur, who watched in the rear view mirror. The men settled back in their seats for the short ride to the upscale restaurant.

The big car glided to a stop at the curb minutes later where Paul watched as the car drove from sight, then he went into the public house.

"Paige?" Tony asked as a telephone conversation began in another part of town.

"Good morning Tony."

"Can we talk, over coffee?" he asked.

"We're talking now on the telephone," she answered.

"I can't see you over the telephone. I want to look at your lovely face as we talk," he responded softly.

Hearing his remark sent a thrill through her, "You know we are in an impossible situation, we can't be involved! Not even as friends," Paige said.

"Have coffee with me and we will kick around the pro and con of this, situation, as you say. No touching, I just want to look at you. If we can't reach an agreement, I won't call you again for at least two days." Tony said.

"How about Mel's near my apartment?" she said and laughed.

"When?" he prompted.

"Is an hour all right?"

"See you there in an hour." He said, as the connection was broken.

In the lobby of Mel's café they walked across the space between then. There was that certain kind of warmth when two charismatic people were together and conversation wasn't necessary. They were shown to a booth in a secluded corner.

He deliberately sat on the same side with her and had a close up morning view of a fresh-faced young woman. She moved into the curve of the seat,

"I'm glad you came," Tony said softly.

The waitress arrived for their order.

"Coffee, make mine black," he said, turning to Paige, inquiring, "Paige?"

"Cream and a sweetener," she said.

The waitress went away.

"What do you know about this feud?" he asked.

"Not much. I ask mother and she told me our fathers were best friends once. In fact they were inseparable, and after the University they went across Europe on a shoestring and then into business together," she answered.

The coffee arrived and the waitress arranged the cups sugar and creamers then left, saying, "Enjoy."

"I've always known the feud was there, but we never talked about it, the servants would snicker about it from time to time. So, what happened after the business blow up?" Tony asked.

"There were losses in the beginning, and my father does not like to lose. They had numerous arguments during their association. Then there was one major fight after a big loss, and they have never spoken again except to yell at each other or to get ups-man-ship in business, and in the news," she answered.

"Messy situation, and through the years they have been sniping at each other always trying to get the upper hand. This thing has taken too much of their lives and now it's interfering with our happiness," he said.

"Tony, you forget I'm engaged," she protested.

"Break it he's not for you," Tony said, in a matter of fact way. He searched her face, saying, "I'm more your type. Meeting you was like coming home where I belong."

"Have you been talking to June? Did she have something to do with our meeting on the tennis court?" Paige asked.

"No, I've met June once briefly should I talk to her?" he asked.

"Of course not!" she exclaimed in a loud whisper.

"Seriously he's not for you, and you know that." He paused momentarily, then said, "Now that I have found you, he can't have you. I have always known you were somewhere close by," he said softly and touched her hand. "I have searched for you and I won't lose you to anyone."

"We were babies when I saw you last," she said.

"I didn't realize we had shared a diaper changer," he said facetiously. "I knew we were meant for each other the first night we met again then we danced and I was hooked. We will be great together," he whispered intimately.

"Now really!" she said with quiet indignation.

"When we kissed it was all over for me. Just holding you in my arms, the taste of you, and to feel the warmth of your body against mine. You felt it too, admit it," he responded softly.

"Tony, I … I please!" she stuttered. Paige felt trapped, and intensely aware of his masculinity.

"We were meant for one another. I don't care about the damn feud, our fathers and certainly not Ashley. He is all wrong for you and he can't have you," he said again softly.

"I should have something to say about that," she said.

"You have everything to say about it because I'm planning to marry you in the not too distant future," his response was assured.

"I think I had better go, this is getting out of hand. You have us married already. Tony get on the same page with me. I'm engaged to Ashley," she repeated.

He gently turned her face toward him and lightly touched her cheek with his fingertips.

Their eyes met and once more they were drawn to each other.

He whispered, "I know, I want you and I am here to tell you with candor. I plan to have you for my wife."

"Now you have us married?" she asked.

"I insist on it," he answered.

She had to tear her gaze away from his.

"Will you tell Ashley or should I?" Tony insisted.

"I have to go now," Paige said. "I need space to think! I have to go!"

Before she could leave, he said gently, "The only space I need is one with you and me in it." And touched her hand.

Paige moved quickly around the booth.

"I'll call you," he said as she practically ran from the café.

He followed more slowly, leaving money for the untouched coffee.

In Paige's apartment she threw her hand bag on a chair and kicked her shoes across the room then plopped on the couch and dialed the telephone, Paige said, "June I need to talk to someone and you are elected."

"Something wrong?" June asked.

"Not really," Paige answered

"What's up girl friend?"

"I just had coffee with Tony Jordan, and he has some wild idea that he is in love with me. He went so far as to say he was going to marry me, in the near future." Paige said.

"Wow, my kind of guy! Where did he tell you this?" June asked?

"Mel's, not a half hour ago," Paige answered.

"I was hoping it was a ritzy hotel room, and he jumped your bones and screwed your brains out." June said and giggled. "But, things are looking up! Don't you feel something for him?" she asked.

'Yes, I do feel something for him, more than I care to admit. After he kissed me. he's in my thoughts constantly I can't get him out of my mind, it's crazy," Paige said, "But you both have forgotten Ashley."

"I can forget Ashley without trying, and you should too, he was born old." She paused, then said, "Paige dear, we have to look at this objectively. I ask you, would Ashley ever in your wildest dream take a chance on never seeing you again by telling you he has fallen in love with you and was planning to marry you in a public place like, Mel's?"

"No, of course not. Ashley would never do that, but June, Ashley does have some good qualities. You are about as objective as a sock in the eye, and you are saying Ashley is different." Paige said.

"There's a concept. You know, I was probably stolen from the palace at an early age." June said and laughed."The things you have said proves my point, you need Tony. A red blooded, virile young man to hold you in his arms, plant lip bruising kisses on your mouth and any other odd places, and anytime," June said.

"He can certainly do that, his kiss sent my senses sky rocketing, but life goes beyond charm and sex appeal," Paige said.

"It helps. Tony is my kind of man! I love it. I love it!' June said happily, then asked, "Did Ashley ever kiss you with his mouth open?" June asked.

"Never, he would never do that! You nut," Paige said giggling.

"See, case closed. I told you he has an odd hemorrhoid pucker that probably goes all the way back to his puritanical beginnings," June said.

"I will discuss it when Ashley is in town," Paige said.

"Don't talk about it, break it off. Do it cleanly and never look back. Believe me Ashley will survive. You need Tony, take it from me go for it girl friend."

"You're no help. June I love you but I have to consider this carefully. I will call you later." Paige said and gathered her purse and shoes and went to her bedroom.

She sat at the computer and deleted page after page of script, then she roamed around the apartment, saying to herself, "Calm down and weigh the pro and con of my relationship with Ashley. Can I face a lifetime with him and his stuffy friends? Actually June is right he is not mister excitement for a young man. Now Tony, is certainly more spine tingling than her courtly fiancée. Paige had begun to realize she wasn't truly in love with Ashley. June was right about that, too. Paige had to smile at that picture, June being right. But one does not live by thrills alone. Was Tony the right one? He has certainly been in her thoughts a lot, and he has persistence. Was her attraction to him physical or could it be the beginnings of a true love? Questions crowded her brain.

Paul Unger, a dapper dresser, and skillful fixer of deals entered the Cavanaugh mansion late in the evening.

He and Benton were examining a volume of papers, with their drinks at their elbows.

Paul said, "This is probably the rule of law we should go with," then he sipped from his glass.

Benton took the papers, saying, "Let me see that," and looked through the pages making faces as he read. Then said, "Paul I think you have it," as he turned back a few pages to recheck something. "We will go with this one. Look at this clause," he said, pointing to a particular section on the page.

Paul read it, answering, "Yes … yes, I can see the possibility. This should do the job nicely," he said, after reading the passage.

Benton paced around the room rubbing his hands together in anticipation, saying, "Paul, this is better than having a woman the first time," his exuberance was hard to restrain.

"Will that be all for now Mr. Cavanaugh?" Paul asked, as he packed papers in his briefcase.

"You have gone far beyond excellence this time, I can always depend on you." Benton said.

"I try my best, sir." Paul replied.

"Make the proposal in the morning," Benton said.

"I set the appointment tentatively for tomorrow at nine depending on your approval," Paul answered.

"Keep it," Benton said as he walked to the liquor cabinet, "This calls for another drink, what were you having?"

"Bourbon on the rocks."

Benton brought the drink to Paul.

Connie came in, stopping just inside the door.

She said, "Paul, how nice to see you again. It's been a long time."

"It's good to see again too, Mrs. Cavanaugh I have been busy recently," Paul answered.

"Yes I can imagine. Benton is a stickler for hard work," she said.

"I am accustom to hard work Mrs. Cavanaugh."

Benton was in an expansive mood and poured her a glass of white wine, saying, "Paul, when this is all over you deserve two weeks off with pay."

Connie turned to look at her husband, because he never gave time off with pay, unless he was making lots of money.

"Take the two weeks and the bonus Paul," she said.

"Connie, my dear Connie even you can't spoil my evening," Benton said and laughed.

Paul sipped his drink and prepared to leave.

"Oh Benton, shame on you." Connie said playfully.

Paul stood, saying, "Sir, I will have to go now."

Benton shook his hand, "I'll expect a call tomorrow as soon as you're done."

Paul nodded as he left the room with Benton and Connie in close conversation.

CHAPTER 8

♦

During the same space in time Tony had tried repeatedly to reach Paige.

Maggie entered the room.

"This is Anthony Jordan, may I speak with Paige Cavanaugh please." he said.

The maid answered, "Ms. Cavanaugh is not available, sir."

"When will she be available?" he asked.

"I'm not at liberty to say, sir."

"Thanks," he said and turned to Maggie, saying, "Maggie, I am afraid I might have frightened Paige."

"You came on too strong. Tony, you can't do it that way."

"Tell me about it, I can fix it if she will only answer the telephone,"

"Don't call, go talk with her face to face." Maggie said.

"You may have a point there. I have to absolve myself with her. Maggie, I can't lose her now that I have found the right one." He said. Worry lines creased his handsome brow, as he leafed through the telephone directory then dialed a number.

"Clyde, Tony here. I want you to send a dozen red roses every four hours throughout the day to Paige Cavanaugh, the Seton Towers west. Do it every day until I tell you to stop."

Tony went into the meeting room for the conference of the day, and sat across from the others.

Kenneth had his feet on the table.

"The schedule for the tournaments are buttoned down tight." Tony said, "Omar is on his way to the U.S. Open and rising faster than any of us anticipated."

"His line of clothes is grossing thousands. Omar is on his way to being a multi-millionaire and he is handling it well, too." Avery said.

"You didn't do so badly yourself, but that's enough about business it makes me hungry. How about dinner?" he asked.

"I'll call Maggie," Tony answered and turned to an intercommunication button to the kitchen, saying, "Maggie."

"Yes my dear Tony," she answered cheerfully.

"Come in here please." He said.

She appeared moments later with a feather duster in her hand, she looked at Kenneth, and said, "Get your feet off that table Kenneth I just cleaned it today."

He took his feet down immediately then used his hand and shirtsleeve to clean away any dust that might be there.

"Now, what can I do for you dear?" Maggie asked.

Tony laughed and said, "Dinner, how about, Moo-Shoo Gai Pan, Garlic shrimp, soup and salad. You know what to order."

"Dinner. You got it. No pork it's bad for my blood pressure. How many are eating?" Maggie asked.

"Six, ask Omar to join us," Tony said.

"Better make that seven servings," she said, and looked at Kenneth pointedly. "Is that it? This will only take a little while. I'll ring when I'm ready."

"How is your budget holding out?" Tony asked.

She held up a circled forefinger and thumb, "Very well."

Maggie ran the feather duster over the surface of the table and looked meaningfully at Kenneth.

He shrugged his shoulders under her stare when she shook her finger at him and left the room.

"You give her a budget?" Kenneth asked,

"And what is wrong with that, Kenneth?" Maggie asked, peaking around the door.

"Ah … nothing, a good idea, I might do the same thing," Kenneth said.

"I'm gone for real this time, talk all you want Kenneth, bad mouth me, enjoy yourself," she said as she moved away.

Kenneth shrugged his shoulders again, but was quiet…Tony was returning from an early morning practice session. When he came around the corner of the hedge, and stopped in surprise.

Paige was driving up the drive and parked a short distance from him.

"I came to tell you, I think you have sent enough roses, the children's hospital is full." She said.

"Come in and have coffee with Omar and I. Later I'll show you around the compound," he invited.

"I would like that, and to see Omar again, thanks," she said as he opened the car door and showed her inside.

Omar turned as they came in, and said, "Paige? Paige Cavanaugh, you sassy little devil! How the hell are you?"

"The one and only you ole sweetheart. Come here and give me a hug." She answered.

Omar gave her a squeeze and swung her off the floor.

Tony looked on in incredulous surprise.

"Tony, I didn't know you knew Paige," Omar said.

"The subject never came up." He said.

"It did once," Paige said.

"She was my buddy at the Country Club sit ins," as they walked to the counter with their arms encircling each other.

Tony poured coffee.

Omar said, "None for me, caffeine is bad for my body." Then he turned to Paige, saying, "It's been great seeing you again, but I have to get a rub down. You come around to see the boss more often, so I can say hey to yah."

"I might do just that," she answered and laughed.

Omar kissed her on the cheek and left the room.

"Well, will wonders never cease. You have more dimensions than I ever imagined. How's the coffee?" he asked.

"Very good, you remembered," she answered.

"Maggie does something special with coffee and she never tells me the secret," he said.

"Would you show me around this wonderful place?' she asked.

Maggie strolled in as they were leaving.

Tony said, "Maggie, this is Paige Cavanaugh. Paige, Maggie is one of the thousand points of light in my life."

Maggie held Paige by the shoulders, saying, "I would know this child anywhere. I took care of her when she was just a baby, now she is all grown up. How are you doing?" she asked smiling.

"Hi Maggie it's good to see you again. Mother spoke of you often when I was growing up," Paige answered.

"And you grew up so pretty, how are your parents?" she asked.

"They're always the same." Paige said.

"I have to go now honey, my boss-man keeps me jumping," Maggie said in a loud whisper, "Bye Tony," as she left the room chuckling.

"It seems everybody knows you but me. I'll have to remedy that," he said.

"On with the tour, Sir Tony," she said jokingly.

He showed her outside and in a circuitous route through the courts, stopping to watch an early morning practice session, the gymnasiums, weight rooms, pools areas, and dining rooms centers, the kitchen and other sights until they arrived back at her car.

"I also wanted to tell you, that you and June were right about Ashley and me. I plan to tell him when he comes back to town," she said.

Tony turned her around and gazed at her, several seconds, then said, "If I take it slowly, could we have dinner and dancing later, a jog or something?" he asked.

"I can't promise you anything now it's too soon. I had hoped you would understand," she replied, climbing into her car.

"It's just a jog around Promenade walk in the morning," he suggested.

"I could do that as a matter of fact I would like it. I'll see you on Papasian Way at six a.m. sharp. I run well and I need to see what you got," she said smiling. As she backed out of the parking space then drove away.

Their days were spent laughing in the market place, talking, jogging, cycling on the beach and dinner and dancing. He took her home afterward.

Tony said," Paige, we have many things in common and being near you makes my day. May I kiss you good night?"

"Yes, I would like that," she answered.

He held her face lightly between his hands and kissed her soft mouth sweetly and sensuously to begin. Then her arms crept around his neck and his around her waist drawing her closer to him. He was consciously aware of the lines of her soft body yielding against his. The kiss was getting out of hand when she pushed his away breathlessly, saying, "I have to go inside, Tony," in a shaky voice.

"It's fate for you and I to be together. Face it, it's inevitable," he whispered.

"Ashley will be back soon, I still have to tell him my decision. That's the honest thing for me to do," she answered.

"I'll tell him." He said.

"It's my responsibility I'll do it. I have to go inside now Tony, really, and I have to make another admission to you."

"What is that?"

"Your presence is very comforting. Thanks for so many lovely days, and for being so understanding," she said.

"I will call you tomorrow, okay?" he asked softly.

"Yes. Oh no, I have a script meeting out of town. I'd better call you when I return," she answered.

"I'll be waiting," he said, and kissed her lightly and lingeringly on the lips. Then went to the elevator and waved to her as she went inside her apartment.

More than two weeks had gone by and Tony had not heard from Paige. His repeated calls had been declined. He sent flowers everyday still no answer.

Her maid had a list of rebuffs, Ms. Cavanaugh is indisposed, she's out, or not taking calls every kind of maddening rejection.

Tony talked to Omar, saying, "I have tried everything to talk to Paige, but

I don't get any response. I'm in love with her, what can I do?" he asked in frustration.

"You've called, sent flowers everything? Stop doing that, you've done the courting bit, go over in person have an up close and personal talk to her. Sometime women like to be swept off their feet. You know kissy face, cuddle, whisper sweet nothings in her ear things like that," Omar said.

"I can do that, how did you get so smart? Sort of a frontal attack so to speak, but in a nice way." Tony asked, as he made his departure.

"You got it," Omar said.

Paige sat on the terrace in early twilight reading, surrounded by large arrangements of flowers.

Catherine her maid came out followed by Tony, saying, "I am sorry Ms. Cavanaugh he wouldn't take no for an answer."

"That will be all Catherine, thanks," Paige said as she stood to face him, "Tony, I thought you would wait for my call? I received the flowers as you can see."

"I came because I couldn't take anymore rejections," he said,

"besides, you weren't taking calls. I had to apologize for intimidating you on our first time out for coffee." He said.

"You didn't frighten me. I needed space to think because between you and my friend June I couldn't concentrate. I had to face some truths in my life and know where I'm going," she said and found herself looking into his incredible blue eyes, fringed with long lashes, set in a face tanned by the sun. His stare was so disconcertingly hypnotic she had to tear her gaze away.

"Have you made your decision?" he asked.

"That's my concern don't you think?" she replied.

Tony held her shoulders, saying, "That's not the question. Are you clinging to Ashley for some ethereal reason? Maybe the need to suffer? You can't marry him you don't love him. Your response to me tells me otherwise."

"Yes, I have known for some time, but couldn't admit it to myself. Things were happening fast, too fast with you!" she said, vehemently. "I've gone over this situation in my mind and viewed all the pitfalls," she stopped speaking for a moment, "I know now, I'll break the engagement with Ashley because I really never loved him, and I still haven't resolved the problem with our parents."

Tony started to speak, but she stopped him.

"No please, let me finish. I have carefully reviewed Ashley and my lifestyles, and the thought of living in the Smith mansion was too much for me to face for a lifetime. Then you came along, an unknown quotient that didn't stay unknown for long."

"Paige, I'm totally and unabashedly in love with you, and I want to spend the rest of my life proving it."

Her resolve weakened, "I can't deny my growing feelings for you in the times we were together."

Tony drew her to him; "Our love will grow stronger," as he planted soft kisses on her face and mouth.

"On Tony," she breathed his name. His nearness thrilled her as she was caught in the flames of desire, she let her arms slowly encircled his neck as their kiss became profoundly intense..

Tony buried his face in her hair; "I have never felt like this about anyone. You and I belong together, you must know that." He said softly.

Uncertainty gripped her, and she pulled away and walked to the rail to stare into the distance, "Tony, can this actually happen so soon with two people?" she asked.

"Believe it, it happens," he answered.

"You are a different aspect to enter my life. You're on my mind a lot, your presence makes my head spin like, too much wine," she admitted, "But is that enough?"

"It works nicely for me. I have fallen in love with you, it's that simple," he said as his eyes devoured her face.

His voice saying the words electrified her. Page was speechless, then stammered, "But, but I ... I"

"I knew it when we met. You felt it when we danced, admit it," he coaxed softly.

"Yes I did, but I need to be certain! It frightens me, I could be wrong," she said, then changed the subject. "Would you like a drink?"

"Paige, sweetheart there are no absolutes in life," he said gently. "I don't need a drink, it's you I love, you are holding our life in these hands," as he held hers in his.

"I have to tell Ashley," she said.

"I'll tell him, where is he?" he asked.

"No. It's my responsibility," she said.

"When?" he asked.

"He returns tomorrow night, I will tell him then," she answered.

They faced each other, and were drawn together like two magnets, their touch was electric. The kiss was long and emotionally unsettling.

Paige's feelings of wanting him spread through her. She had to tear herself away, and said, "This is too fast. Too fast!" knowing there was no turning back.

"Apparently I didn't do that right, let's do it again," enfolding her in his arms, he thoroughly kissed her soft wet mouth, sensuously slow, as the warmth spread to his loins. Paige entwined her arms around his neck.

When the kiss ended, she asked, "Will you kiss me like that fifty years from now?"

"This can only get better, and better." He said and laughed.

"If that's a promise I'll hold you to it." She said,

"Piece of cake," he said and kissed her face.

"What took you so long to convince me?' she asked.

"Didn't want to frighten you away." Tony said softly.

'Take me to bed," she whispered.

He carried her to the bedroom and kicked the door shut and between lip bruising kisses they undressed each other in their rush to strip away the encumbrances if the past . The flames of desire spread and consumed them as he touched her smooth skin. He guided her to the bed and tossed the covers to the floor.

Paige's arms encircled him as he laid her naked among the pillows and trailed kisses down her throat to her shoulder and the valley between her bosom cradling her breasts in his hands. Her nipples hardened as he fondled them with his warm wet tongue, tantalizing her senses with every touch. He tasted her body until she was wild with desire.

She felt every titillating thrill as her hands moved over him, touching, arousing, their emotions and his enthralling all consuming energy.

He entered her slowly, and sensually as he made love to Paige. Tongues tasting as both uttered cries of pleasure while his strokes went deeper, faster and more jarring. Their young bodies gleamed with perspiration as their skin made wet sucking sounds when they made contact and then parted.

Their satisfaction was complete when they reached climax.

They breathed quickly as his body settled momentarily on her then he rolled away satiated.

He hugged her to him savoring the feel of her moist body, he whispered, "If this goes on for a lifetime I'll die happy."

She smiled as they snuggled closer. Paige fell asleep to the muffled beat of his heart.

CHAPTER 9

◆

In KISG's television studios, Avery Markyme sat across from his guest. "My visitor tonight is Mr. Benton Cavanaugh. Mr. Cavanaugh was kind enough to grant us this interview," Markyme turned to Benton, "Congratulations on your acquisition of the Bison football franchise."

"Thanks, Avery," Benton said and grinned, his smugness was clearly evident.

"It was rumored that you and your competitor, William Jordan were bidding for the same team," the newscaster said.

'Yes, I heard that same rumor," Benton answered, as his grin widened.

"Was this coup just the luck of the draw?" Markyme asked.

"No, this was based on research and sound business principles," Benton responded.

"Where do you go from here, sir?"

"I have more ideas, you will know in time," Benton replied.

"You heard it here first ladies and gentlemen," Markyme said, preparing his closing.

"All my business dealings are done from research and logic," Benton interrupted rudely, "No chicanery and no crookedness in my business dealings!" His outburst was fiery.

Avery was surprised, and continued hurriedly, "Yes, yes I'm sure they are," then turned to the camera with a smile, "That's all for this hour, stay tuned for the nine o'clock Sports Round-up with Tom King.

Benton reluctantly uncrossed his legs.

During the late evening news Benton sat before the television.

The newscaster said, "And now for the news on the home front. The engagement of Ashley Boregard-Smith and Paige Cavanaugh has been canceled . Mr. Smith had no comment as he boarded his jet for Europe today."

"Did you know about this, Connie?" Benton asked and turned the television off by remote control.

"No, it's news to me dear," Connie said, with the usual distant reply.

"Why would she do that? After that damned expensive engagement party last year," he said.

"I have no idea dear," Connie answered.

He stood and started to pace then stopped in front of his wife, and asked, "I have heard rumors. Is she seeing that Jordan boy?"

"Call her Benton, " Connie subjected.

He mimicked his wife, "Call her Benton, I'll do just that!" he barked and yanked the receiver off the hook and jabbed angrily at the numbers on the phone pad, and waited impatiently then said loudly, "Catherine I want to speak to my daughter!" He jammed the receiver down moments later, "I knew that apartment was a mistake!" he muttered as he paced.

"Benton?" Connie said.

"Living alone was a damn fool idea! No telling what goes on over there." Benton said as he stopped pacing and stood beside his wife's chair.

"Well what did she say, dear?" Connie asked.

"Your daughter isn't there, not there! Probably out gallivanting with that snot nosed boy of Jordan's!" Benton said as he stormed out of the room.

Maggie was in the kitchen chopping vegetables as she listened to a television news broadcast. The announcer said, "Paige Cavanaugh and Anthony Jordan are the children of the two feuding conglomerates. Well folks the offspring's have found each other and have been seen about town for intimate little dinners, dancing cheek to cheek, the theater and other places. Is this the item to watch? We will keep you posted ladies and gentlemen."

Maggie laughed loudly, saying, "Way to go Tony! Man, I would like to be a fly on the wall to see old man Cavanaugh turn red over this!" she laughed again, "That would sure be a grabber." she laughed and turned back to her vegetables.

The object of all the news, Paige and Tony were lingering over coffee in a secluded patio booth where the lights were low and soft music played in the background.

He took her hand in his and kissed her fingers, and whispered,

"Paige sweetheart, my love for you grows with each passing moment. I have no other way of saying this, except to say I want you to be my wife, will you marry me?"

Overcome by his tenderness, she answered, "Tony, are you sure this will make you happy? I would be heartbroken if you ever had any regrets."

"I have never been so sure of anything in my life," he answered as he took a jewelers box from his pocket, "Will you marry me? This marriage, I insist on it," he repeated softly as he opened the box to reveal a sparkling solitaire engagement ring.

"Oh yes," she breathed happily and admired the solitaire when he slipped the ring on her finger.

It sparkled in the subdued lights, "Our love can only grow," he whispered.

"Yes, yes, yes!" she said as he savored her kiss.

"You know our families won't like our getting married, it'll be difficult," he reminded her in a sobering moment.

She held his face between her hands, whispering, "I am marrying you, we're marrying each other not our families, we will be family."

"Absolutely. Just you and me, I like that. We can't let this happiness pass us by," he said.

Paige kissed his face, a show of affection in public, something she would never have done in the past. She liked the idea, saying softly, "You are all I need, and as you've said, I insist on it."

They kissed again sweetly with tenderness, lost in their own world.

Diners at the nearby tables smiled their approval then applauded.

Men gave him the thumbs up when the lovers turned around.

Tony sat across from his father with his legs crossed days later.

William's voice rose in anger, saying, "Anthony, I have read very disturbing news about you and Paige Cavanaugh you have been seen everywhere together."

"It's no rumor. I love her and plan to marry her as soon as possible," Tony announced.

His father's mouth fell open, he had lost his urbane air, and William's next verbal delivery was less than courtly. He bellowed. "I forbid it! A Jordan wouldn't be caught dead in the company of a Cavanaugh and never, we would never marry one!" He said the words as if they left a bitter taste in his mouth.

"Forbid?" Tony shot back, "That's forceful language coming from your Dad."

"Yes, I said forbid! I repeat, no Jordan would ever be caught dead with a Cavanaugh!" William shouted.

"This one will and love every minute of it!" Tony snapped, "Paige, isn't marrying my family, she's marrying me!"

"Don't use that tone of voice with me!" William ordered, and rose half out of his chair, "If you marry her, you are no longer a son of mine!' he sputtered, "I'll take you out of my will! You, will be disowned!"

Tony was momentarily stunned; his father's words were like a fist to the solar plexus. "I am sorry you feel that way dad because I will always be your son. As for the money you forget I have enough of my own," he said pointedly.

"A tennis bum?" his father scoffed then sat and turned his back angrily. "When you marry her you are no longer a member of my family!'

Tony looked at his father's back, and said, "You said that and slammed the door on our relationship. I am being married to Paige. You will know when, I would like you and mother to be there but, If not, so be it."

His father squared his shoulders angrily, and did not answer.

Tony left the office and closed the door softly.

William's secretary Kim had heard the argument and mouthed the word, "Bravo," then made applauding movements with her hands when Tony waved to her.

The doorbell rang repeatedly at June's apartment in the evening. When she opened the door Paige hugged her and danced into the room.

June was taken aback, "Well that was some entrance, what is the occasion?" she asked as she closed the door.

"I am engaged," Paige said then held her hand out with a queenly pose.

"Paige! It's gorgeous!" June squealed. Then she sobered, saying, "You did this before, to whom are you engaged this time?"

"Tony of course. June it was so romantic," she swooned.

"Say no more," June said as she pulled Paige across the room, "Sit right here and tell me every delicious detail and don't leave anything out," as she pushed Paige on the couch then plopped down herself and hugged a throw pillow to her chest, squealing, "I have goose bumps! I am so delighted! Go on tell me, tell me, tell me!"

"We had dinner with wine, soft lights and music," Paige said, starry eyed, "He held my hands and actually kissed my fingers in public." She paused, momentarily, "June, it was so beautiful then in the candlelight he said he loved me and wanted to marry me. He said, he insisted on our marriage."

"Oh my goodness, I think I am going to faint!' June said and fell over backward on the cushions holding her heart.

"Don't you dare faint before I'm finished," Paige said and threw a small pillow at her friend.

"Go on! Go on then what?" June asked as she sat up.

"He slipped the ring on my finger, and said he loves me more every day" Paige said.

"I don't want to raise sour grapes, but what about your parents?" June asked.

"Who cares, this is our life and I love it," Paige answered more cavalier than she really felt.

"You're damn right it is," June said.

"I remembered something you said to me." Paige said.

"What was that?" June asked.

"That I needed someone to make mad passionate love to me anywhere and anytime," she answered.

"Paige, you didn't!" June squealed again.

"Didn't we and it was wonderful. Ashley called before I broke the engagement during one of our intimate moments," Paige responded.

"You are lying!" June cried.

"He didn't recognize the throws of passion when he heard it. He, ask me if I was all right. Tony couldn't stop and I didn't want to either. It was great! Now you can faint," she said as they hugged each other giggling.

There was a panoramic view of the ocean and beyond from the terrace of Toney's beach house.

He and Paige were splashing each other in the surf then they ran laughing breathlessly to the house.

On the patio their eyes devoured each other as he held her in his arms, and her hunger equaled him.

She said coyly, "I am for a shower won't you join me?"

"By all means let's … you spicy little Chile pepper," he said standing aside with a courtly bow and laughed as she swished through the door with Queenly Aires. She dropped her bra top on the way. He hopped along after her stripping off his swimming trunks Inside the sumptuous bathroom a full-length window overlooked a rock garden and farther out to the Pacific Ocean.

Under the full spray in the shower they soaped each other, hands gliding fluidly over the contours of their bodies, chest and buttock. He held her slippery body in his arms, saying, "I have a woman with a logical mind, and a body that's, … ," then he breathed in through his teeth and exhaled, continuing, "Unbelievable."

"You said you knew you loved me the very first time we danced? Really?" she asked as she leaned back in the circle of his arms.

"Absolutely. Why do you think I wanted to dance with you, to hold you close like this," he answered.

"We had just met," she said softly.

"Maybe I was remembering the diaper days and I am a little partial to older women," he said.

"Flatterer." Paige said.

"You were so beautiful, and seeing you there so untouchable. It didn't take long to know that we were destined to be together," he said kissing her throat.

"Bored was more like it. I am glad you came along in time to rescue me," Paige replied.

"So am I, and I like the change from bored to adorable," Tony said.

"It was a pleasant surprise for me, too. I found you weren't the ogre the media said you were," she giggled.

"I have always been just a pussy cat," he said softly into her ear as her nipples hardened against his chest.

Paige moved closer with her arms around his neck with the full length of her wet body pressed against his. She kissed him passionately arousing him more. Their bodies came together because of their insatiable desires and great sex.

His hands cupped her hips holding her close while her hands flowed over his erogenous areas. They moved out of the shower and he lowered her to the soft white rug on the bathroom floor as the flames of desire consumed them.

He smothered her face with kisses down to the curve of her throat.

Their lovemaking took on an overwhelming urgency that sent their senses soaring. She uttered cries of pleasure and she wrapped her legs around him as their mating absorbed them.

Tony exhaled releasing a breathy sigh when they reached climax together. When the fires of their ardor was appeased they gently dried each other and he carried her to the bedroom where they climbed between the cool sheets.

Benton in the Cavanaugh home was watching the end of news as Connie read her book nearby.

The newscaster said, "Paige Cavanaugh and Anthony Jordan are inseparable. Is this the item to watch? I think so ladies and gentlemen. And other tidbits to watch, is it love, for June Sawyer. She has been seen around town with a certain police officer, John Jacoby. It seems when love blooms it touches all of us, Omar Stevenson has been out with the lovely Jacquelyn Donner. We will keep you updated as all the news unfolds."

"What is this rubbish with Paige?" Benton asked fiercely as he turned the television off.

Connie was engrossed in her book, "What rubbish, dear?" she asked.

"She is still seeing that Jordan boy!" he yelled.

"Pat and William's son?" she asked.

"Pat and William's son," he mocked her, moving his head from side to side, then bellowed, "Of course that crooks son! Weren't you listening?"

"That's probably the reason she broke the engagement to Ashley," Connie answered absently.

He looked at his wife in exasperation, "That is obvious Connie! But I will put a stop to that right away!" he shouted and started to pace the floor.

"Paige is of age, Benton," she answered as she followed his movements around the room with a pained expression on her face.

He whirled around, yelling savagely, "No daughter of mine will be associated with a jackal like Jordan!" he said shaking his fist in the air.

"Calm down dear, you know your blood pressure can't stand the strain," Connie said,

"Damn that now, Connie!" Benton barked. His face was growing red as if his collar was too tight.

"That problem with William should have been over years ago. The idea, of two grown men fighting for the last twenty years is ridiculous. It is impossible for me to understand, Benton," Connie said.

"It will never be over as long as he lives in this town!" he said.

"Benton, really! I will call Paige and have her come over. You two can discuss the matter, calmly," she replied.

He interrupted rudely, saying, "No waiting around with this Connie!" he changed his course on pacing and stormed over to the telephone, and yanked the receiver off the hook then jabbed at the button pad savagely then waited impatiently, he slammed the telephone down with a clatter. Then said, "I hope you are ready, remember we are meeting the Horvath's at eight," Benton said over his shoulder as he went out the door without a backward glance.

CHAPTER 10

◆

In the posh La Maison Roux restaurant lobby, Benton approached the checkroom. A tall man with his back to him turned and bumped into him.

"Excuse me," William said. Absentmindedly.

When they recognized one another Benton stiffened, and snapped, "I want that whelp of a son of yours to stay away from my daughter!"

"My son, is too good for a Cavanaugh!" William snarled.

Benton stood to his fullest height, his face growing red, he sputtered, "Why you, you, you low down rascal!"

"If there's a rascal around you should know, you are the jackass!" William shot back

"No Cavanaugh will ever link up with a Jordan again! If I can help it!" Benton shouted.

"You are asking for another black eye, and a fat lip!" William yelled.

"You won't sneak up on me like the last time, come on and fight like a man!" Benton said raising his fists. They circled each other like bantam roosters with their fists raised.

A group gathered, and the press loved it. Connie and Patricia looked on miserably

The manager intervened, saying, "Gentlemen please! Could we take this into my office?" he asked, as Benton's punch slammed into his jaw. The manager fell into the gathering crowd.

"No!" William yelled, "I'm leaving! Come on Pat!"

Patricia winked and smiled at Connie, then drew her wrap around her shoulders, saying, "Coming William." Pat was lithe and had the long legged walk of a model and a mind of her own.

Connie raised her eyebrow and smiled at her old friend, as Pat swept out of the lobby.

When Benton was settled in bed, Connie sat beside the telephone and dialed.

Paige rolled out of Toney's arms.

She answered, "Hello, Paige here."

"This is mother, dear."

"Hello mother."

"Paige, I want you to come to the house and talk to your father," Connie said,

Paige sat up apprehensively and threw the covers back with her feet on the floor, "Is he sick?' she asked.

"No dear but you should talk with him about the news reports," Connie replied.

"Why?" Paige asked.

'There was a fight between your father and William Jordan tonight at La Maison Roux, and your dad is extremely upset," Connie said.

"Mother, upset is nothing new, if it's not urgent I will come over tomorrow," Paige promised.

"It's not that pressing, but you should come as soon as possible, sweetheart," Connie said,

"Tomorrow. I love you mother," Paige answered.

"That will be fine Paige. I love you and you'll always be my angel face, no matter what. I will see you tomorrow, dear," Connie replied and smiled as she replaced the receiver.

Paige turned to Tony.

"What?" he asked.

"My mother the peace maker. It seems my father was upset about something in the news," she paused momentarily, "My father, and your father had a fight tonight in the posh La Maison Roux."

"I'll go with you," he said as he balanced himself on one elbow.

"That will cause more problems. My dad's bark is worse than his bite. I can always manage with him," she said reassuringly.

"We knew it would come to this, although I didn't anticipate a fight in a public place," Tony said and chuckled.

"I am glad in a way, and a little angry, after all this is our life," Paige said.

"I'll drive you," he said.

"Oh darling, I love you for saying that but I'll be all right," she said, with more conviction than she felt as she snuggled closer.

His voice was muffled against her body, "Tony, I am so lucky to have you."

He looked at her and lightly moved a tendril of hair from her face, "Somehow your father thinks of me as a rock that has learned to speak," he said jokingly. Sobering he continued softly, "I love you so much it hurts. It wounds me just knowing you may be unhappy because of your love for me," He caressed her gently. "I can't let you go alone. I'm mad about you and want to take care of you." He held her as they lay in one another's arms.

"Make love to me,' she whispered.

"That I can do," he answered, drawing the sheet over their heads.

"And you have my vote anytime, you do it so well, too, "she giggled, There was laughter under the sheet, "Tony! You devil!"

"And don't you forget it," he said as sounds of kisses ensued.

The next day Benton stood before the fireplace looking down at his daughter, "What is this I hear about you and this Jordan boy?" he asked.

"What did you hear?" Paige asked, her eyes were defiant.

"It is in all the tabloids! You're all over town everywhere with him! What do you have to say for yourself?" he asked tersely.

"It's true," she answered.

"Is that all you have to say?" Benton demanded.

She looked into his eyes, then retorted, "Yes."

He shook his finger in her face, "You will not see him again young woman!" Benton ordered.

Paige was taken aback by his vehemence, "This is my life, daddy!" she answered hotly.

"We Cavanaugh's haven't spoken to a Jordan in over twenty years," he yelled.

"Daddy, is it my turn to live now? Mr. Jordan was you friend, that's your loss. That's a long time to be angry with someone. It's about time you both got over it," she answered angrily.

He slammed his hand down on the mantle, bellowing, "I will spell it out for you! You, will not see him, again!"

"Or what daddy, you will disinherit me?"

"Yes!" Benton snapped, "I knew this was a mistake for you to move out on your own. June did this, she was always a strange child."

"You forget grandfather's will, you can keep your money, daddy. We won't need anything from you. And further more June is my friend and she didn't persuade me to do anything."

Benton sputtered.

Paige said, "I will not relinquish control of my life, because of a senseless feud. Neither of you really remembers why it all started."

Benton raised his hand as if to strike her, she stopped and looked levelly at her father.

Then said, "Daddy, really now."

He lowered his hand and turned his back. "You will be sorry, the son is like the father, he will leave you, too." Benton warned.

"That happened between you and Mr. Jordan, daddy."

"Don't come crawling back to us when he leaves you! Now get out!" He exclaimed, "This is not longer your home!'

"I will! Good-bye daddy," she replied and ran from the room.

Benton winced as the door slammed behind her. Sorrow showed on his face as he leaned his forehead against the mantle and a tear escaped down his cheek.

Tony met Paige at the beach house door; they embraced and walked to the couch then sat together.

"I have never had a fight like that with my father," she said sadly.

"Your father feels as if he's losing you. He will come around in time," Tony said with more assurance than he felt.

"Daddy actually ordered me out of the only home I have known all my life." Paige said as tears flowed.

"It happens to the best of us," he responded.

"Your father, too? I never had a clue, why didn't you tell me?" she asked,

"I didn't want you to be upset. You know I never knew much about this damn feud until you and I discussed it. My dad was different, too when we had our shouting match." Tony said.

"It is ridiculous to think someone would hold money above friendship, or love." Paige said softly.

"I never knew all the details," Paige said and started to weep, and Tony drew her closer. "It never really concerned me. Oh I didn't live totally in a vacuum, the servants gossiped. I heard rumors about some business deal that went wrong and they lost money, and then there was the feuding over the years," he said and tilted her face up, "We will be happy together and after our fights there will be the making up period."

"Yes, I know that," Paige said and tried to smile, then tears started to flow and Tony kissed them away.

She continued, "'Tony, sweetheart, I need to get away for a while to think."

"Because of the feud?" he asked.

She held his face gently between her hands, "No. It will only be for a week. I have to sort things out for me, no for us. Please sweetheart don't say no," Paige appealed to him.

"I don't want to lose you not even for a moment," he answered.

She touched his lips with a forefinger, "Our love will endure, we know that now, I'll be gone a week," she said, "And don't you try to forget me."

"You will call?" he asked.

"Not for a week sweetheart," she stood to leave then said softly, "You are my weakness, and I have to go now or I'll never be able to walk out that door," Paige kissed him fervently then touched his lips with a finger. "Keep my place." Then she hurried away without looking back.

There was a grieved expression on his face as he started to follow her, then he stopped at the door and leaned his forehead against the doorframe.

Alone in her dressing room, Patricia Jordan dialed a number, and relaxed against the cushions of in her chair.

Connie answered on the second ring, "Hello."

"Connie, Pat here, can we talk?"

"It has been a long time." Connie said.

"Too, damned long but we can remedy that if you are agreeable," Pat suggested.

"I would like that very much it'll be like old times Pat."

"Are you busy this afternoon?" Pat asked.

"No, not really."

"Connie can you meet me at the Tearoom?"

"On Van Ness?" she responded.

"Yes, say about one-ish?" Pat said.

"I will be there, see you then," Connie said as the connection was broken.

In the old world setting of the Tearoom where the atmosphere was quiet and the service impeccable, dating back to the time when people of gentility played Crochet on the lawn.

Two old friends met and embraced as if they had just seen each other the week before.

When seated, Pat said, "How do you feel about this damn feud our husbands are still carrying on?"

"I thought it would be over years ago, " Connie answered. Then said, "Now Benton has fought with Paige. He said she is not allowed in the house. You and I know he doesn't mean that. Actually he's always a push over for his daughter."

"The same thing happened with Tony. William said he would disinherit him but he hasn't done that, yet. Actually he is hoping Tony will come back eventually and ask Williams forgiveness. I found him staring out the window, so forlorn. When he saw me he pretended he saw movement on the lawn."

"It's so good to see you and to be able to talk to you again. I didn't realize I had missed you so, until I saw you in the restaurant the night of the fight. We should never have waited this long," Connie said as they held hands.

"I know, our husbands are such fools all this time wasted over a silly misunderstanding," Pat answered.

"In a way we compounded the problem," Connie said and stopped speaking momentarily. "Although, we never went as far as the foolish part. Pat, you know how it is time goes by and things happen when you are caught up in daily living."

Pat nodded, then said, "Now they are trying to ruin our children's life, what are we going to do about it, Connie?" Pat asked.

"We cannot let that happen." She answered.

"We won't let that happen," Pat was vehement.

"You know the kids are going to be married?"

"Do you have any reservations about them being married?" Pat asked.

"No, I want them to live happily without interference from the jackasses we are married to. Even though we love our husbands dearly they have to be made to see the light before it's too late," Connie answered.

"We agree on that part and I plan to participate in the wedding in any way I can," Pat breathed a long sigh, then said, "I am starving, tea is all right but how about some lunch?"

The luncheon was very pleasant; they talked in animated pantomime until late in the afternoon, as if the past years had never happened while they lingered over coffee, "You will call me next week?" Connie asked.

"Yes. I am delighted we could talk, but I have to go now," Pat said and looked at her watch.

"'It's better late than never. We will stay in touch," Connie said.

In the parking lot they hugged then climbed in their cars and drove away.

A.J. Enterprises was at the point where Tony had the freedom just to keep watch over all transactions with daily reports and updates.

Omar Stevenson was riding a winning wave, and could not seem to lose. Through the weeks of play he had netted money and growing prestige, and his following bought his line of clothes.

Aunt Evelyn was one of his staunch supporters and had become a fixture at his matches.

In his off-hours he was busily starting a clinic for younger people who wanted to learn the game in his neighborhood.

The surf was rough, buffeting the shore. Paige stood momentarily to watch Tony as he sat gazing over the Pacific. He turned slowly when she waved. They started to walk toward each other faster and faster until they were running along the beach then together hugging and laughing happily.

He crushed her in his arms and whirled her around off the ground.

Her arms were around his neck when he stood her on the sand.

"I couldn't stay away any longer," Paige said breathlessly. "My car drove itself back to you. Your face, this face that I love so much haunted me everywhere I went, there were reminders of you."

He squeezed her, and in a harsh whisper, said, "Smart automobile I was ready to look for you. I missed you and we can't do this again."

She leaned back in the circle of his arms, saying, "During this week the only thing missing was the real you. I lusted for the warmth of your body against mine and your arms weren't here to hold me like this."

He buried his face in her hair, saying, "Umm you smell so good. I love you so much more every day, don't close me out of you r life. If you leave again I will find you."

"You can't get rid of me now, if you want to change your mind it's too late," she said playfully.

"Forget it, I missed you too much and I want you with me always," he replied.

"I love you so," she said, as she hugged him around his middle, "I had to think because of my argument with daddy. I know now I can't live without you," as they walked toward the beach house.

"I was always sure so where do we go from here?" Tony asked.

"Promise me one thing." She said.

"What's that?" he said.

"We will discuss anything that arise and never fight about our fathers because I love my dad. I have forgiven him for a lot of things he does. June and I always thought he was a little nutty and so funny when we were kids." Paige said.

"I agree. My father and I had some great times together. My accident really brought us together. And mom, has always been a kick, down to earth, kind of a rebel with a mind of her own." Tony said.

Paige looked up at him, and said, "Now we have to make plans for the wedding," as they walked to the house.

Weeks later in the evening they sat on the floor surrounded with books on weddings, bridal gowns, lists and everything that dealt with nuptials as soft music played in the background.

Paige answered the knock on the door to allow June and John Jacoby, Brooke Topplinger's and Clive followed by Omar with a date. Kenneth, Eric Prendergast and a number of other friends arrived along with caterers bearing food and wines.

Their greeting was boisterous and friendly with hugs and lots of smooches.

Brooke bustled in and lived up to her reputation. She was drop dead gorgeous in a black low cut little number.

"Don't get up we will serve everybody. Clive is here and he is the best at that sort of thing," Brook said and turned to Clive and the caterers that carried dinner. "Just put it over there on the counter and table. I brought paper plates. I hope you don't mind paper plates but we don't like doing dishes, do we Clive?" she stroked the grinning Clive and tossed her purse and jacket on the floor beside the couch.

Clive and the caterers set up and served dinner. When Brooke leaned over to attend to those on the floor her bodice was hard put to contain her voluptuous bosom.

Tony said, "Brooke, mourning becomes you dear," and kissed her on the cheek.

"The wedding is on I see," Brooke observed, then leaned closer and said softly, "You two belong together, it was always my choice."

June came over, and said, "I met Omar and this gorgeous lady, Jacquelyn Donner downtown, and persuaded them to come along."

Kenneth swaggered over, "I gotta say you folks have some good looking fillies in this town," he said and slapped Omar on the back and checked Jacquelyn out, "Marvelous, it's good to meet you Jacquelyn save a dance for me."

"You're very kind, thanks, I'll do that," she answered.

"Kindness has nothing to do with it, you are a dream come true." Kenneth said. "Clive says so, and he knows," Brooke said.

"Welcome, I'm glad to see that Omar isn't all play," Paige said as she hugged Jacquelyn and Omar.

"Tony kissed her cheek and hugged his approval," saying, "Where did you meet this ravishing woman, Omar?"

"At state two years ago. We had lost touch until recently, Jackie had an athletic scholarship, too," Omar answered.

Paige said, "This is my best friend take good care of him."

Omar and his usual easy going self laughed.

"I'll do just that," Jackie replied.

Kenneth played a rhythmical tune and couples cleared a space to dance. Omar and Jackie joined them and swayed to the music.

Clive came over, and asked, "Is the wedding still on?"

"Yes, the wedding is definitely on, and the sooner the better," Tony answered.

Brooke said in a whisper everybody could hear, "I told you she was the one for you, remember?"

"This was my best decision," Tony replied.

"Where will the ceremony be held?" Brooke asked.

"We haven't decided, yet." He answered.

"Don't bother to think about it. It will be at my home in the lower terrace with the waterfalls and mirror ponds in the background, and tons of flowers." She looked skyward and said with a catch in her voice; "It'll be so romantic. Clive and I will take care of everything," She stopped speaking and turned to Paige and June, then to the whole room of people as she hugged Paige, saying, "Darling, your wedding will be held on my lower terrace, and I won't take no for an answer. You have to let me do this it's all settled. Clive will take care of all the particulars, your colors everything, with your approval of course. He is good at that kind of thing, trust me. It will be so wonderful!" Brooke said all this without seeming to take a breath, then clasped her hands together ecstatic with anticipation.

More friends arrived, one said, "We heard there was a party."

There were groups dancing, eating, and lots of laughter, conversation, and a few brave souls went for a dip in the pacific surf and ran back shivering.

The impromptu party lasted until late in the night.

"Wait everybody before we leave, and since we will all attend this wedding. As you know, today the big wedding is in fashion, with engraved invitations the whole enchilada," Brooke said.

June burst in, saying, "Banks of flowers, engagement parties, formal rehearsal dinners and bridal showers."

"The bachelors party, you must let Clive arrange that!" Brooke said as she put her arm around Clive's shoulder, "He does everything so well, don't you love?"

Clive could only grin as she volunteered his services.

"I, will take charge of the brides maids I need the practice,' June said, as she looked up at John and hugged his arm.

He gazed back at her affectionately.

The feeling of spontaneity was infectious they all wanted to get into the arrangements.

Kenneth shouted from the rear of the room. "I am the groom's best man, and I know a great minister. We gotta get these people married. I just bought a new limousine perfect for the wedding."

"We need public relations, the press will have to be there, and the reception won't be a gala without a good dance band," Brooke said.

Eric Prendergast, yelled, "Leave something for me we will need committees and great lists, limousines for the families and trusted friends etc. Why don't we take telephone numbers tonight, and arrange the committee members later. Just let me know what group you want to work with," he said, all in his best British accent.

The preparations and planning had taken on a life of its own. The young women were grouped around with the bridal magazines, they oooo'ed and ahhhh'ed and compared the lovely gown's.

Paige and Tony sat back and marveled at their friend's enthusiasm.

"A young couple today," Brooke said and turned to the potential bride and groom, "That's you, and you must be ready for the whole kit and caboodle. The wedding is categorically, culturally and traditionally the brides show, it's her day."

"Here! Here!. It takes hard work, and it requires tact and great management skills of which I am well equipped to do." June said.

"Paige has the last word in all things," Brooke said. "Let's toast a wonderful couple may they live and prosper, and make love a lot." The assembled group drank amid the laughter.

"When is the wedding?" Kenneth yelled.

"Three months." Paige said.

"Make that two months," Tony corrected.

Paige and her ever present check lists flitted from one fitting to another must do appointments as the weeks went by. Engraved invitations were sent. She and Tony spent most of their evenings together. They sat on the floor facing each other. Her legs straddled his thighs with her feet curled toward his backside. Paige had her arms around his waist with her face on his chest.

"Tony I need a hug," she said, "I have been debating about sending our parents an invitation, should I or not?"

"Yes, I think they should know the wedding date, and they are wanted there with their blessings," Tony answered holding her close.

"Do you think they will come?"

"Our mother's maybe, our father's are too stubborn to give in so easily," he answered, moving his hands gently over her back and said soothingly, "If they don't want to be a part of the most important day of our lives, we have each other."

As if trying to convince herself, she said, "Our marriage will be good, won't it?"

"It will be the best don't doubt it," he said softly as he tilted her face up toward his, "We will have our problems although they won't be like most people. No financial difficulties our relationship is based on love, and mutual respect."

"What about divorce? It happens," she asked.

"Don't think it we won't ever go there, never," he replied vehemently.

"But sweetheart, we need to discuss everything no matter how unpleasant. We should weigh any and all possibilities," her voice was muffled against his chest.

"Yes I know but no talk of divorce," he repeated.

"And about my list, my half is taken care of. Brooke and Clive are doing a wonderful job on their portion. All that's left is the wedding rehearsals and the rehearsal dinner. The songs and choices of singers are on your desk for your approval when you want to talk about them. Your best man, and would you ask Omar to give me away? Lastly we need the license and blood tests, " Paige responded.

"Omar will be pleased I'm sure he will do it," Tony said.

"Did you know Clive is really good at this sort of thing?" she asked.

Tony laughed.

"No really, he has everything ahead of schedule," she said.

"I am glad you are pleased," Tony said.

"He shouldn't be a houseman, he should do weddings and special events," Paige said.

"I heard Brooke say," Tony mimicked Brooke, "Clive is good at this sort of thing." They laughed and he squeezed her tighter, then asked, "Why Omar?"

She leaned back in his arms and gave him a quick kiss on the lips then ticked her reasons off in her fingers, "I have grown to like him very much, and he was so adorable in diapers dragging that tennis racket sucking the pacifier. He is down to earth and could have been the brother I never had, and because Omar won the grand slam in the last tennis tournament. Besides, he is handsome and perfect for the job."

"Good answer. I will ask Omar, and we will discuss the songs later," he said. "So, you saw Aunt Evelyn's scrapbook?"

"Yep, she showed it to me, we had orange juice at the kitchen table and chatted," Paige said, "She likes you, you know. I also saw your stats in the book and you were just as delectable then as you are now. Bad boy of the courts," she said, and hugged his middle.

"That bad boy nonsense was just for publicity," he said.

"If daddy could see me now sitting astride a man," she laughed, "How are you on kissing of late? I haven't had one for a long time."

"Your fault, I tried hours ago but you had a list to check," he said softly.

"I am ready, lay one on me," she said impishly, and he kissed her thoroughly. When it was over Paige murmured, "You do that so well you must have had practice. Do it again exactly the same," The kiss became playful as they rolled over on the floor laughing in a tangle of legs.

<h1 style="text-align:center">Chapter 11</h1>

◆

Benton's telephone buzzed in the limousine, "Benton Cavanaugh," he listened and then placed the receiver down with a pleased expression, he said, "Take me home, Tom." he ordered the driver.

"Yes, Mr. Cavanaugh."

"I have something most men never have in a lifetime," Benton said gleefully.

"What is that, sir?" the driver asked.

"Fulfillment. There is always contentment in knowing one's limitless boundaries," Benton answered and cackled. The driver wheeled the automobile expertly into the stream of traffic.

In another part of town Brooke bustled about wearing a sheer caftan over form fitting tights. Her dress designer had devised a clever method for fashionably containing her ample bust in the thin strapped top that complimented her trim figure. She moved from one place to another with swatches of cloth matching them to the already luxurious surroundings. She turned to her houseman, saying, "Clive, what about this, does it a match?"

Clive spoke with a lisp, and his Café Au Lait complexion was flawless, he said, "Honey, that's just perfect. Wait, let me hold it you can move back for a better look," as he held the swatch.

Brooke backed away shaking her head, "Noooo, not quite right, this has to be perfect. Like you my little chocolate drop, and don't let anyone hear you call me honey. I am the boss. We need some decorum around here, you can only boss me around when we are alone."

"Yeah, right," Clive said, and snapped his fingers at her, then turned to another task.

Brooke went to the pile of swatches, and rummaged through the stack, "No! No! Wrong, wrong all wrong! We only have so much time before the wedding, damn it!"

Clive swished out of the room and Brooke continued to mutter to herself shaking her head and tossing swatches right and left. She called loudly, "Clive! Sweetheart, your gay-ness come here please," as she stared at the last few pieces of cloth.

He poked his head around the door, "What? I am busy you know," Clive replied.

"I want to know about our list how are we coming along?" she answered.

"We're caught up for now," he explained, "All we need are the decorators the day before, the flowers are already ordered everything is arranged. I will call for them two days before. The minister is set," he thought for several seconds with one finger to his chin, then said, "Are you sure you want this preacher he looks so young! Calvin, better still was he old enough to be ordained?"

"Calvin? Of course he was ordained silly, I was there," she answered. "He has modern ideas we don't need some old Fuddy duddy. Kenneth's minister was in an accident and will be out of circulation for several weeks."

"Calvin Grouper sounds like a fish. That's his real name?" Clive asked.

"I swear," Brooke answered as they both laughed.

Connie showed the wedding invitation to Benton when it arrived, she asked, "Are we going?"

"No!" Benton snapped then tossed the envelope on a table as he sat in his chair and noisily opened the Money Maker Daily

Connie tucked the envelope in her book and later dialed the telephone, she asked, "Pat, did you get the invitation?"

"We did, and William is being a silly ass as usual," she answered.

"Same here, you still want to attend?" Pat asked.

"I wouldn't miss it for the world," Connie answered.

"I will call Brooke in the morning you know R.S.V.P., and all that for us," Pat said.

"What are you wearing?" Connie asked.

"Something new and expensive, we will go shopping for a stunning outfit for whatever mothers in law wear." Pat said..

"'Tomorrow, at Victoria's Boutique up town for starters. It will be like old times shopping together again," Connie said.

"I will see you about one-ish," Pat replied as the connection was broken.

Tony opened the door to his office to find his mother looking through an album.

Pat smiled, and said, "It's about time you're getting here I was about to come looking for you." As she closed the album, "Your students are amazing."

"Mother, what a pleasant surprise. Why didn't you call I would have been here," Tony said as he walked across the room to hug his mother.

"I watched that fantastic young man practice. Omar is all that's been said about him, and more." Pat said and kissed Tony on the cheek then wiped the lipstick off.

"And, he is getting better," Tony said.

Patricia leaned back to look at her son, saying, "Love becomes you, I approve."

"Did you get the invitation?" he asked.

"Yes. Connie and I will be there but your father is another issue. You are both alike, stubborn but I love you both in spite of it," she said.

"Thanks mother, Paige will like that," Tony said quietly.

"How is she holding up Tony?"

"She is amazing." He answered.

"Love her and stay with her. We will be there front row center."

"The press will be there but you might have a problem with dad," Tony warned.

"Leave that to me, didn't you know trouble I like and peace I do despise as

Maggie just told me." Pat said.

"Would you like a drink?"

"Maggie and I had one already, you know she is quite a character," Pat said.

"Yes, she is," he answered.

"I am going now but if you need me you know where I am. Don't hesitate Anthony, call me," Pat said.

"I will mother," he said as they walked toward her car.

Tony stood in the driveway and watched his mother's car disappear from sight. Then he slapped his hands together and danced a little jig as he went back inside.

The private bridal dinner was held at the Ritz Plaza Hotel a week before the ceremony, relatives, and close friends along with members of the wedding party.

Brooke, and Clive had taken care of everything down to the last detail, dinner was superb.

Kenneth said, "I have to practice my toast master skills, how is this? Over the teeth and by the gums look out stomach, here it comes." His southern accent and delivery was uproariously, funny.

"No, no, noooo you can't use anything like that at this wedding!" Brooke said, between laughter. "This is a sensitive occasion. You have to go back to the drawing board quick."

"After that bit of merriment it's time to leave," Tony said, as he helped Paige with her chair, "Kenneth that was terrible."

Dinner was over and the guests were ambling through the lobby involved in jovial conversation, when there was a loud.

"Yoooou hoooo Tooony!" with another hail right after, "Yooou hooo Tooony daarlinnnng!" Janet Claude called as she teetered across the space between them on spike heeled shoes, news reporters and photographers in tow. Her dress clung to every line of her figure. She pressed herself against Tony and planted a wet kiss on his cheek leaving lipstick smeared on his face as the flashbulbs flared. He stood dumbfounded in the glare of the flashing cameras

He backed away in embarrassment a few steps, stammering, "Oh, ah, Janet ah, you haven't met my ah, fiancé, Paige Cavanaugh. Paige, this is Janet Claude," Tony said lamely.

Paige tried to be polite but Janet rudely dismissed her with a curt nod of her head.

The wedding party gathered around along with others from the lobby to see the movie star.

"This takes brass ass nerve!" Brooke protested.

"I thought you were in Europe?" Tony faltered He wished he were far away when he looked at Paige's face who was not pleased as Brooke wiped the lipstick off his face.

"Darling, Europe was a bust. That rat Glenn wasn't the right leading man for me so I came home," Janet raised one arm to display her figure in the best way to the cameras while flashbulbs flared, "Did you miss me?" Janet asked, with a smile.

"As you can see, my wedding party and I are leaving. It's been good to see you," Tony said, as he took Paige's arm guiding her through the door, followed by their entourage, "I'm sorry about that sweetheart," he apologized.

Paige shrugged her shoulders and made a face, "That's why dear, the past has a nasty way of catching up with us, sometime," she said, dryly.

The photographers took pictures of the disgruntled look on Janet's face as she watched Tony and Paige leave followed by their party. Janet stamped her foot then rudely pushed the cameramen aside then stormed out of the lobby.

The morning after headlines read, "Janet Claude, gets the cold shoulder from her former main squeeze, Tony Jordan. The star stopped the Jordan wedding party in the lobby of the Ritz Plaza Hotel last night with his newly betrothed, Paige Cavanaugh. The starlet planted a sloppy kiss on the famed tennis player. This reporter asks the burning questions, ladies and gentlemen, is what happened in Europe between the statuesque Miss. Claude and the matinee idol Mr. Glenn? We have it from someone who knows. Mr. Glenn signed a contract of the decade with Garibaldi of Italia Films. Could he have been so unchivalrous as to dump

Ms. Claude on her shapely derriere. And, does she want to recapture the limelight with the businessman of the year, Tony Jordon?"

Paige lived at the beach house part time until the wedding.

When Tony arrived the next morning the newspaper was spread on the counter. Janet's picture covered a major portion of the front page as she posed to show off her ample figure.

The headlines, "Janet Claude, gets the cold shoulder from her former main squeeze, Tony Jordan."

Tony laid the newspaper aside when Paige came into the room, he tried to kiss her as she adroitly avoided him before he could come near.

"What's wrong?" he asked.

"How long has that, that Janet person been back in town?" Paige asked.

"I don't know. Last night was the first time I've seen her since she practically knocked me in the pool at Brooke's party, over a year ago." he replied.

"Right," she said sarcastically and looked into the distance.

"What does that mean?" he asked.

"Nothing, except she was far too friendly smearing all that goo on your face," Paige said hotly.

"That wasn't my fault! She was always an affectionate little thing, she liked to touch," he said, trying to change the mood of their conversation

"So that was touching I saw last night. Tony, she practically smashed her boobs on your chest!" Paige said angrily.

"Are we fighting about Janet? She means nothing to me," he said, with a little chuckle. "You're the woman I love and you will be my wife, not her!"

"Why did you snicker? This is our future and it isn't funny!"

"Maybe we shouldn't get married!" Paige said, raising her voice.

"And what does that mean maybe we shouldn't get married?"he asked hotly.

"Ashley, would never let her do what she did last night!" she answered.

"That stuffed shirt probably wouldn't know what do if a woman touched him." Tony said, "He didn't touch you, and I'm glad of that."

"I am glad, too!" Paige cried, "He, he was no "Ashley was kind, and, considerate, a gentleman… None of that showing off in public either."Paige said.

"I rest my case. He is a stick in the mud, and so is his whole old world family!" Tony retorted.

"You let her kiss you, and she has a mole! A big fat mole on her lip!" Paige shouted.

"I was told that's a beauty mark, and it's not so big," he said, with a grin on his face.

"I should have smashed her face, and knocked her on her shapely derriere!" Paige said, as she tapped her finger on the picture of the actresses backside on the front page of the paper.

"Paige, it's my turn to talk now! I won't listen to you. I'm leaving before this gets really nasty. I will see you when we can talk sensibly. I love you but I won't argue with you especially about Janet Claude" he said, and waved his hand as he left the room, closing the door softly.

"What's the matter? Can't take the heat?" she said to his back as he disappeared from sight. "Don't bother to come back!" Paige shouted, then fell across the couch, sobbing.

Hours passed while Paige walked the beach, a lonely figure. Finally she went to the beach house and dialed the telephone, when the call was answered, she said,

"June! Tony and I had a fight!" she sobbed

"Maybe we'll have to call off the wedding!"

"Was it because of last night?" June asked.

"Yes!" Paige wailed into the receiver.

"Don't be silly that was nothing. That broad wanted to use Tony for publicity, and that's all, publicity. You saw today's paper it didn't work as she expected." June said.

"But June, she rubbed herself all over him, and he's been gone for hour's! June I've spoiled our life, everything is ruined!" Paige cried."It's so late maybe he's hurt!"

"Don't be foolish he's okay. Janet, took a shellacking in Europe now she's licking her wounds and trying to get some recognition by using Tony, last night. She did it before he met you," June said pointedly.

"I could have wrung her neck if she'd had one, she's all chest Paige said trying to smile as she dried her tears.

"You tell Tony you love him, and he is the best thing that's happened to you. Whisper sweet nothings in his ear, and screw his brains out. That will fix it," June instructed happily.

"I can do that, thanks friend," Paige said as they hung up the receivers.

Tony had not gone to the academy, but had driven to Twin Peaks on Outlook mountain and sat for hours deep in thought and at times he threw rocks into the gorge, finally he went to the camp to talk to Omar.

He said quietly, "Paige, and I had a fight this morning about that crazy Janet Claude. I have been t loose ends for hours wondering what to say to her."

"Why is she upset? We all know that whole scene was for the cameras," Omar answered.

"Janet and I were involved before I met Paige," then hastened to say, "But I haven't seen Janet for months!"

"Well, she did wrap herself around you like tape last night, "Omar replied.

"She was always that way a little seductive, you know touch-y -feel-y," Tony said.

"Man, her actions last night said in no uncertain terms come on over Tony, and rescue me," Omar said, chuckling.

Tony spoke as if he had not heard, saying, "I haven't thought of Janet since she broke off our relationship."

"I'll bet she loved the publicity that kiss got her it was all negative stuff," Omar said.

"Yep, she said any exposure is good publicity you just need to be there. She liked that kind too," Tony said.

"This is my sage advice, tell Paige that you love her and her only throw yourself on the sword, so to speak. That usually does the trick, women love that stuff," Omar spoke with seeming authority.

Tony looked at his watch, saying, "It's kind of late to call her now."

"If I were you I would go to Paige tonight, and tell her up close and personal how special she is in your life. Tell her how much you love her, sweep her off her feet. Time doesn't matter, man. And, remember you heard the following here first. 'Anytime is the right time to be with the one you love'. Trust me, it works," Omar said.

"That's a song," Tony answered, "Paige said you were a wise young man. That's why she wants you to walk her down the aisle and give her away, can you do that?"

"Me? Wow!" Omar said and laughed. "I would be happy to walk her down the aisle and give her away."

"I will remember your sage advice, thanks Omar."

"You can take credit for my being able to help the kids in my community. I wouldn't have been here so soon without your help." Omar said.

"No, you are where you are because you are able, and it's due to your efforts, and your great athletic ability. I am just the conduit by which you arrived at this point in your life," Tony said, pausing, "Omar I think I will take your advice, I'm going and claim my woman, tonight. How do I look," as he stood, and adjusted his jacket.

"Looking good! Way to go Tony!" Omar said, giving him a double thumbs up.

"I will see you later," Tony said, as he jumped down from the bleachers and walked to his car with a buoyancy in his steps he did not have when he arrived.

Paige heard the tires of his car crunch to a stop in the driveway, then she followed his footsteps as he walked down the path to the door. His key grated in the lock as she sat up on the couch.

She ran into his arms when he opened the door. saying, "Where have you been? I've called everywhere! I thought you were hurt!"

"You can see sweetheart I am all right. Oh honey, don't cry I'm fine," he said, embracing her gently.

"I was worried sick it's been hours!" as tears flowed down her cheeks, "I thought you were unconscious somewhere!"

His hands caressed her then held her in a rib crushing hug.

"Tony say you will call me if we fight," he couldn't get a word in as she kissed his face.

His voice was muffled in her hair as he ,whispered, "I love you. I love you, I love only you."

"Let's not fight anymore," Paige said, "We will find something else to do like bungee jumping, or sky diving, anything."

"That would do it for me it scares the hell out of me just thinking about throwing my body and yours from heights like that," Tony said, laughing.

"Me too," she said and laid her face against his chest. "When you walked out that door I had this terrible feeling in the pit of my stomach, and I must admit, I was jealous of her."

Tony lifted her face with one finger under her chin and looked into her eyes, saying, "Seriously, we can't quarrel. I love you too much to hurt you by arguing, and recrimination. Sweetheart, you must remember this, Janet really never meant anything to me. That was reinforced that last night," he kissed her nose. "I know she was using me for one of her publicity stunts but I can't be without you. This has been the loneliest day of my life, I thought I had lost you."

"Not a chance," she said.

"You are my light, my life. I have been going crazy the past hours because I couldn't hold you like this. To reassure you and kiss your mouth, and see your face up close and special," with merriment in his voice, saying, "I'll be glad when this old fashioned wedding is over then we can get rid of those damned lists."

Paige hugged him around the middle as they walked. They lay sleeping later as she snuggled close with her face near his chest, and one leg over his thigh. He slept with one hand on her bottom and the other arm supported her head.

◆

Chapter 12

The wedding took place on Brooke's estate, in the early afternoon right on time. Brooke and Clive had constructed an open gazebo secluded near the vine covered mountainside, abutting the stream and waterfall in the background where the scenic remoteness, and privacy was accentuated. In the middle of a clearing stood the gazebo with its altar carved in wood and set atop stone. It was decorated artistically with blossoms, the most ideal setting for the ceremony.

At this time in the spring the shrubbery was a lush rich green with wild flowers in full bloom. Behind the clearing was view of a steep hill ascending to the second waterfall level in the distance. The quiet soothing sound of the stream and falls could be heard quietly beneath this rustic scene, swans glided across the mirror ponds everything united with nature.

The mothers of the bride and groom were video taped when they arrived and seated in their place of honor complete with tissues.

Video operators, and still photographers took a vast assortments of pictures. The band played softly in the background.

The guests were assembled. Tony and the best man Kenneth crossed over the bridge that spanned the stream and down the path to wait at the altar, while the brides maids followed.

The strains of the traditional wedding march sounded, and then Paige and Omar appeared and slowly crossed the bridge into the clearing.

There was an audible gasp from the audience when the bride came into view as she and Omar moved majestically along the path.

Her gown was of the purest white with an overlay of lace trimmed with pearls around the hem and bodice. Her veil and train required four girls to carry it down the petal strewn path.

Omar was strikingly tall and handsome in his tuxedo as the sauntered slowly beside Paige.

Calvin Grouper, the minister started the ceremony, saying, "Dearly beloved we are gathered here in the name of, God In the face of this company to join this man and this woman in holy wedlock. The estate of matrimony is not to be entered lightly but reverently, solemnly in the sight of God. If any man can show just cause why this man and this woman may not be joined in holy matrimony let them speak now or forever hold their peace."

No answering voice.

The minister, continued, "I say to you Anthony and Paige if there be an impediment why you should not be joined together in holy wedlock that you confess it now."

The video cameras rolled, and still pictures were taken.

No answer.

The minister, began, "Anthony will you take this woman to be your wedded wife, to live together according to God's holy covenant in the sacred estate of matrimony? Will you love, honor and keep her in sickness, and in health? And forsaking all others keep yourself only to her so long as you both shall live?"

"I will," Tony answered.

Tears escaped down Patricia's cheek as she grasped Connie's hand, and yanked tissues to dry her eyes.

Connie was enthralled and breathed a sigh.

Brooke stood aside, caught up with the solemnity of the ceremony as she dabbed at her cheek with a dainty hanky.

The minister turned to the bride, saying, "Paige, will you take this man to be your wedded husband to live together according to god's holy covenant in this sacred estate of matrimony? Will you accept him, love honor and keep him in sickness and in health? And forsaking all others keep yourself only to him so long as you both shall live?"

"I will," Paige said quietly as their eyes devoured one another's face Who gives this woman to be married to this man?"

Omar caused to be joined the left hand of Paige to Anthony for them to plight their troth.

Connie sniffled and dried her eyes, then whispered, "Oh Benton, you've missed the best day of your life."

The minister, instructed, "Anthony, repeat after me. I, Anthony Jordan, take you Paige to be my wedded wife. To have and to hold from this day forward. For better, for worse, for richer, for poorer in sickness and in health. To love and to cherish till death do we part. According to God's holy covenant. I pledge to you my troth."

"May I have the ring, please?" the Minister asked.

Kenneth searched all of his pockets nervously then with a long sigh of relief passed the ring to the minister. Tony repeated after the minister, "With this ring I thee wed, with my body I thee worship, and with all my worldly goods I thee endow In the name of the Father, the Son, and the Holy spirit. Amen."

The minister, said, "God bless this ring that he who gives it, and she who wears it may abide in thy peace," he said turning to the bride.

Paige repeated, "With this ring I thee wed, with my body I thee worship, and with all my worldly goods I thee endow. In the name of the Father, the Son and the Holy spirit. Amen."

The minister, said, "God bless this ring that she gives it, and the who wears it may abide in thy peace. By the power vested in me, I now pronounce you husband and wife. You may kiss the bride."

The new husband and wife kissed and moved to the bridge. where Paige tossed the bouquet over her shoulder.

There were squeals of pleasure when Brooke caught the spray of flowers. Momentarily she held them to her bosom, then said. "Everybody! Everybody, the reception will be held on the main terrace, dining room, and patio area. Eat, drink, dance and be happy!"

The bride and groom embraced their mothers.

Paige said, "Mrs. Jordan, I'm so happy, I love him so!"

Patricia held her new daughter in law, and kissed her cheek,

"You kids have my blessings that's all you need, my approval," she said.

Connie stood away from Tony as they stared at each other, she smiled and touched his face, saying, " The last time I saw you, you were in rompers. Now you're a handsome man, and my dear son in law. Welcome to the family, Tony," as they embraced.

Inside the dining room, Clive presided over the service of the superbly catered food. His friends had done themselves proud.

The waiters were impeccably dressed as they carried trays of hors d'oeuves, rare wines and the bar flourished. Those who wanted a sit down dinner were served along with the mothers who sat at the table of honor.

The upper terrace had been converted into a temporary dance floor.

Electricians had created a starlight effect.

The bride and groom set the tone with their first dance. They whirled around the dance floor at a dizzying pace. Their laughter could be heard as they danced by. Brooke watched dreamily, saying, "They make a perfect couple," then sighed as she held on to Eric Pendergast's arm while they looked down at her and smiled, Brooke continued, "It's so beautiful," she said drying her eyes.

"Come, dance with me," Eric asked.

"I thought you would never ask," she said as they stepped out on the dance floor.

Other couples followed, Kenneth bowed from his waist, saying, "Mrs. Cavanaugh, how about us tripping the light fantastic?" when they moved to the floor.

Connie proved to be quite a good dancer.

Omar created a stir when he danced with Patricia Jordan. Both were tall and lithe as a couple created a spectacle as they moved gracefully in unison around the dance floor, laughing and talking in pantomime. Their next dance was more lively, a rhythmical tango as the other couples moved to one side to watch, the dance ended to applause.

Still news reporters scribbled and the television news photographers noted every detail of the day with relish.

The afternoon and evening was spent delightfully. It was the pleasure of being with people who knew how to have fun.

There was laughter, hugs and kisses when the wedding party saw the happy couple off on their honeymoon.

William was waiting for Patricia when she returned from the ceremony. She hummed a tango under her breath, danced through the door into the living room.

"You attended that wedding!" he said angrily.

"Yep, I sure did, and there were reporters and lots of pictures. I am sure you were watching. I enjoyed every delicious minute of it," Pat said, with abandoned, and continued to dance.

"Stop that dancing, you went against my wishes!" William responded bitterly.

"You bet your sweet bippy I did. Anthony is my son, too, and I wouldn't have missed that wedding for the world. I hugged and kissed my son and my new daughter in law. She was a beautiful baby and she grew up to be a lovely young woman. I wished them all the best life has to offer,"

She did another dip then Pat gloated, "I danced with Omar, a gorgeous young man. Dancing is something you and I never do any more, and I might don't have fun anymore either."

"I never thought my own wife would turn against me!" William barked.

"I am Toney's mother for God's sake! And I didn't turn against you! I attended my son's wedding to a lovely young woman." Pat answered.

"I am not a blob of protoplasm who does whatever her husband directs her to do, and I never will. That, is why you love me."

He turned away, and smiled when his back was turned, then snapped, "They're not welcome in my home!"

"You forget this is our, home William. They don't have to come here to visit. I will see them when and if I want. But you're right we won't argue about that. I have had more fun today than in the last several years with our stuffy friends," she said swaying to the music in her head. "I can still cut a mean rug and I did that this afternoon, with Omar. That kid, not only can he play great tennis he can dance, too." She pranced a happy tango.

William frowned then slammed out the door.

In the Cavanaugh library, Benton didn't know because he never reads the daily newspapers, and for once he had not watched the television news, he read the Money Makers Daily.

Benton said, "I know now how the coup was done."

"How dear?" Connie asked.

"That Eric Prendergast sold out." he said.

Connie looked at him with a pained expression.

"That son of a sea coaster, a never do well sold me down the drain. He inherited a large block of stock in the Cray ton Company."Benton said.

"Oh Benton, really?" she replied, "He is the son of an old friend."

"He could have come to me," Benton muttered with ill-temper.

"Could he really have come to you, Benton."

Connie asked.

He didn't answer, but stood and took his coffee into the next room.

Connie sighed and followed her husband.

The honeymoon took the newlyweds to places halfway around the world. To Italy's La Scala to see Puccini's La Boehme. In France the Moulin Rouge. In England they toured the pubs, and the palaces just as any tourist would. They walked in the marketplaces, holding hands, discovering, viewing spectacular scenery, speaking sometime in quiet intimate unison.

Tony and Paige were elated when Omar made number four in the world, and immediately telegraphed their congratulation, then drank a toast to the talented player.

The newlyweds arrived to a reception of friends and media.

The mothers meetings at the tea room became a Weekly occurrence.

Connie sipped her tea, saying, "Do you get the feeling that we are the only rational ones in this mess?"

"Yep. I have had that feeling a number of times over the years. But, one gets involved in daily living time passes and that's how we lost touch," Pat said.

"Now that we have found each other again we cannot let that happen anymore. It has been so good just to dance again so free, no pretense," Connie said, as she patted Patricia's hand. Then said, "Benton came home early today, and I had the feeling something was up. He was actually nice to me."

"What do you think happened?" Pat asked.

"He had that, cat that ate the canary look," Connie replied.

"It sounds like William when he has the upper hand on some poor slob," Pat laughed.

"Careful now, that poor slob was probably Benton," Connie said, and they had a laugh at their husbands expense.

"Did Benton see the news about the wedding?" Pat asked.

"I knew he wouldn't he reads the Money Maker Daily mostly, and skips the televised news many times," Connie said, then mocked the way Benton said, "No time for gossip," she continued, saying, "Our husbands will learn someday."

"They'll never learn they're too old," Pat responded.

"I'm afraid if they do wake up it'll probably be the hard way," Connie said sadly.

Patricia changed the subject, "I heard from the children." then paused momentarily, "Remember us when we were crazy in love for the first time?" she asked.

"Yes, those were the good times." Connie said.

"We will have them again, I don't know how but we will," Pat predicted.

"Never like those times but it could be good again," Connie said,

"Our kids are happy it's really very beautiful. Did you see them in the news when Omar went up in the ratings?" Pat asked.

"Yes I did. " as Connie took out an envelope, saying, "Let's compare pictures of the honeymoon."

They shared their photographs and chatted.

CHAPTER 13

♦

Tony came into the bedroom early in the morning and looked down at his wife of five months as he shed his robe and slipped into bed. He kissed her neck below the ear. She moaned softly then turned sleepily into his arms.

"Uuuuummmm you always smell so good," he whispered.

"Tony, darling," she breathed as they kissed hungrily, fanning the flames of desire while their bodies fused in passion.

When the ardor of lovemaking was over Paige rolled out of bed and hurried to the bathroom. He stared in bewilderment after her and momentarily heard her retching then flush of the toilet. Tony came into the room as she rinsed her mouth and bathed her face with a cool wet washcloth.

Tony said, "It couldn't have been that bad."

"Sweetheart, there's something I need to tell you," she answered.

He gently touched her back, saying, "Are you all right now?"

"I'm fine, and the news is you're going to be a daddy," Paige answered.

Surprise, disbelief, then happiness crossed his face. Tony picked her up and whirled her around then remembered, and set her gently on her feet, and solicitously, he asked, "Did I hurt you? I'm sorry, can I get you something?" as he guided her back to the bedroom.

"No sweetheart, I'm just pregnant really I'm okay," she responded.

"What can I do?" he asked.

She turned to him and laughed then caressed the worry lines on his face.

"What! What did I say?" he continued baffled.

"Oh I love you, and you have done your duty already," she answered.

"When is the baby due?" he asked.

"In about six months," Paige said.

"There are so many things to do I will have to make arrangements for the tournament schedules. You know Wimbledon is coming up about then and I want to see Omar play that one," he said as he planned coming events.

"We can still make it because we're going with you," she said touching her abdomen.

"How? There are your check ups, doctors visits, and heaven forbid any complications all that for us to do because I will be with you through it all," he replied.

"I had a talk with Dr. Tom, and we can network with other physicians in the different cities the matches will play in," she reasoned.

"Can we do that?" he asked. "There are doctors records, you will need someone to help you. I don't want anything to happen to you and our baby."

"There is Aunt Evelyn. Oh yes darling we will do this, I don't want to miss Omar's match either. Besides I am as healthy as any young filly you have ever seen." Paige said.

"Maggie will go along with us to help out she loves to travel, it could work," Tony said.

Paige stood and shushed him by putting a finger to his lips. "That is then, this is now," she said as she sat astride his lap facing him, pressing him gently back on the bed in a playfully sexual overture.

Over the next months there was a montage of activity. June, Paige, and Brooke shopped for baby clothes, furniture, and their friends held the baby shower with mounds of gifts for the mother and the baby.

The proud grandmothers were involved in the color schemes as they went from store to store searching through crowded racks, discovering little caps and bootees, and blankets. They laughed as they measured the tiny clothes on their own chests, remembering when they were young.

Paige was photographed at tennis matches around the circuits, and about the city.

The grandfathers moped around in the background as they surreptitiously devoured the news, and photographs in any form they could find but were too proud to join in the delights of grandparent-hood.

Benton and William had started to watch the tournaments from behind closed doors for a glimpse of their off springs. Benton noted Toney's protectiveness. He saw the gentleness and love between the young couple as he guided Paige to and from places. The father's pride in their children was manifested when they were alone, they took pride in their children's popularity

In her sixth month Paige was heavy with pregnancy as she and Tony stood in the newly decorated nursery set aside for the new arrivals. Two baby beds set in their respective spaces.

"Two. baby beds?" he asked surprised.

"I thought I told you the scan showed there are two little bodies in here," she said, touching her swollen belly with her finger tips.

"I'm glad you finally told me because I couldn't take a surprise at the last minute," he said and he hugged her shoulder as they took the last look at the nursery. "You're sure it's two?" he asked.

"Yep, I saw the little critters myself, two cute, tiny, little bodies all curled up in there," she said pointing to her abdomen.

"Come on, you need to sit down and rest," Tony said and closed the door, "Wimbledon is a week away. Maggie can stay here with you. I'll be back as soon as the matches are over," Tony said.

"Sweetheart, darling Tony I am fine there's no way I will miss that match. Omar will blow Sergio away, and I will be there to see it. I still have twelve weeks. If it will make you feel better we can have Catherine come along."

"Stubborn woman. Come on, I need a seat after that bit of news," he said as they walked along the hall with his arm around her shoulder and her arm around his waist.

"I am expecting and not a delicate maiden. I am as healthy as a light weight wrestler," Paige said, "I'm glad you're here, there are so many things to do before the happy event."

"Painting and scraping can't be good for you what if you had fallen?" Tony asked.

"I would get up and make sure I hadn't made a mess," she said. "Tony, these babies are as healthy as little colts," she said and placed Toney's hand on her belly for him to feel the children move.

"Hey!" he said and laughed.

Paige said, "Besides I need the exercise, and so do they."

"Just the same you will be careful, Maggie can help." he said.

"Tony, sometime you are overly concerned, and Maggie can always supervise." Paige looked at him with a twinkle in her eyes, "Of course, there is another way for us to exercise together," she said softly.

"Really, what way would that be?" he asked/

"I have a yen for you so take me to bed and we'll explore our options," she answered.

"I am scared of you, you tasty little wench," he said and laughed.

She put a finger to his lips to shush him then lead him to the bedroom where hungrily and with mutual passion they undressed each other between kisses. Their clothes made a trail across the floor. As they lay in bed tongues flicked between open lips and touching erogenous zones. He held her voluptuous breasts in both hands taking first on and the other in his warm mouth, inflaming and arousing her desires. .

His loin was near bursting when she sat astride him. He uttered a sigh of pleasure then gently held her swollen belly between his hands. their mating was slow, passionate, and sweetly sensual as she rocked smoothly back and forth. He made pleasurable sounds along with her gasp of release as they reached climax..

Visibly shaken Tony held her gently in his arms, savoring the moment as they fell asleep snuggled together.

On the other side of town in the Cavanaugh living room. Benton was reading the Money Maker Daily.

Connie said, "Benton, we need to talk."

"About what Connie?" he asked, lowering the paper.

"Our daughter, is pregnant," she answered.

"Her name is not to be mentioned in this house again ever! She is no longer related to me!" he snapped as his face grew flushed.

"But Benton, she is our daughter, she needs ... "

Benton interrupted rudely, "There is no ifs, ands, or buts about it Connie! The subject is closed! I don't have a daughter!" Benton barked, then opened the news paper with a snap as Connie ran from the room weeping.

Omar was in awe of Wimbledon, the municipal borough of Surrey, England on the suburb of Charring cross, London. It is noted as the site of the, All England Lawn Tennis Club headquarters where international tennis championship matches take place annually. The first matches were held in 1877.

Omar's friends from home along with his following and other people had arrived around the same time filling the stands to capacity. All here to see the relatively new comer who had fought his way to fourth place in the world in a relatively short period of time.

When Omar walked into the court area the atmosphere was electric. He stepped out of his faded over all, and stood there straight and tall in crisp white tennis attire with the ever present bandana. He felt the intense pressure in addition to playing Sergio Wilhelm the number three player in the world. On the court Omar's first serve was explosive. The ball flew over his opponents head, and hit the fence behind Sergio.

Omar murmured to himself, "Settle down now. Settle down it's just a game. We came to play let's do it," His next serve split the service line. The third he tossed the ball up, and it seemed to hang there momentarily then his racket crashed into it as it fell downward, the ball flew into the middle of play. The following volley was spectacular as two razor sharp warriors fought their battle. Stevenson detonated his horizontal serve followed by a blistering backhand.

Wilhelm gave as good as he received as he faced the controlled, relentless power of the ambidextrous and seemingly unwavering Stevenson.

Sergio drove a sizzling forehand cross court.

After Stevenson's crashing backhand there was little time for Wilhelm to get into position before the ball came whizzing back swiftly, and heavy with top spin.

Sergio had no doubt that the man on the other side of the net, was one of the best men in tennis today.

Omar was ready, and he had come to play.

Omar's nervousness had passed, he was in his zone and taking the contest to his opponent, playing the game he loved. He was slightly younger, quicker with longer strides. He hit harder and with more accuracy than Sergio had seen in a long time.

For four and a half hours Omar played every point as if it were vital for the life of this game. He sent top spin lobs, sprinted, and dove for Sergio's smashes. He punched volleys toward the corners, playing the game his uncle had said an athlete should play with perfection. It felt good to be there, this was the place to play, the best grass, the crowds. He carried Sergio from forty love to out. A cross court backhand went by Sergio, laser fast his racket barely moved. Game over. After he shook hands with Wilhelm. Omar fell to the ground on his back with both hands stretched toward the sky. Afterward his trainer tucked a pristine white towel around his neck after he stepped back into his faded overalls.

William and Benton had secreted themselves away in their own private little hideaway to watch the tennis matches. They in their own way were elated when Omar fell to the ground in triumph.

Benton saw Paige and wept his baby was heavy with child, and he was not a part of the happy time of her life.

Outside the English courts the news media gathered at the exit.

The first interviewer, asked, "Omar! Omar two grand slams in as many weeks, and now you have won Wimbledon! How do you feel?"

"I feel great!" Omar said. He was energized and a little winded with all the excitement. He signed autographs while he and Aunt Evelyn moved slowly through the crowd along with Maggie.

One young woman plastered herself to him and kissed him full on the lips. Needless to say Aunt Evelyn and Maggie were not pleased.

"How did you feel going against a player like Sergio?" another reporter shouted over the din of the crowd.

"I was nervous in the beginning then I settled into my game after I warmed up," Omar answered.

"You were certainly up on your game today!" one newsman said, and slapped him on the back.

"Thanks, I played my best," Omar replied quietly.

"After that rocky start your lips were moving. What did you say to yourself in the beginning of the match?" one reporter asked.

"I told myself to settle down, and that I had come to play and do my best against an excellent competitor," Omar responded.

Another interviewer, shouted, "Does your Aunt go to all your matches? She gave you a thumbs up early in the match."

"She and Maggie are the stabilizers in my times of stress," Omar answered, and hugged both women.

"It's Wimbledon's custom to transport the players in luxury cars when they play. The automobile arrived, and purred to a stop to carry Omar's party to their quarters.

This unique consideration by Wimbledon toward it's players as they go to great lengths to treat the contestants like the special people they really are. The Organization has a fleet of Rolls Royce's, Bentley's, and other top quality transportation that's deployed to all participants. Omar climbed inside, and sat beside his ladies and was driven away leaving the media clamoring for any scrap of news they could get for their readers.

Weeks had gone by since the victory at Wimbledon, other tournaments had been played and most were won.

Late one night, Paige sat up suddenly in bed holding her swollen abdomen.

Tony awoke, asking, "What's wrong?" then he saw her holding her belly, and doing Le Maze breathing. He sat up anxiously, "Is it time?"

She could only nod as she breathed in little puffs through the pain.

He continued, solicitously, "It's time for the babies? No, you are early! It's too soon, isn't it!"

Paige kept on with her breathing, and lightly rubbing her belly with her finger tips.

Tony rolled nervously out of bed, "I'll call the doctor," and grabbed the telephone and started to dial with shaking fingers. "What is the number?" Paige handed him the doctors card. He dialed as another contraction gripped her. Paige held her abdomen closed her eyes puffing through the pain.

He waited impatiently as the telephone at the other end continued to ring, then he asked, "Dr. Tom?" Then slammed the receiver down, and declared, "Damn wrong number!"

"Calm down sweetheart," Paige said, then went on with her puffing.

"Easy for you to say," he said and dialed again. His face lit up when the phone was answered, saying, "Dr. Tom, Tony here. Paige is in labor!"

"When did her labor start?" the doctor asked.

"A while ago, seems like hours."

"I want you to time the contraction and take her to the hospital. I will meet you there everything is arranged." Dr. Tom said.

"Yes. Yes I will," Tony said, then slammed the receiver down and smashed his foot against a chair as he hurriedly crossed the room. He limped over and grabbed his pants from the closet then hopped on one foot trying to get the second pants leg on. Finally he nervously pulled his trousers on and zipped his pajama top in the fly. He slipped one shoe on and fell against the wall trying to get the other on huffing, then asked, "Where is the bag, honey?"

"The closet in the nursery," she answered with her eyes closed. lightly rubbing her midsection.

Tony ran from the bedroom, and she could hear him rummaging around, then he yelled, "It's not here!"

She raised her voice, saying, "Look up on the shelf to the right."

He came in out of breath carrying the case and had shoved one arm in a sleeve of his jacket, "Shouldn't you be getting ready?" then he weighed the case in his hand, asking, "What did you pack in this bag, it's heavy."

"Calm down, it's the baby clothes and the camera equipment, sweetheart. You should call for the car," Paige suggested.

"Oh yeah," he said grabbing the house phone, his breathing was ragged as he dialed, then said, "Chester, bring the car around, and hurry!"

"Sweetheart, get my jacket please," she asked.

He dashed to the closet, and rummaged through the clothes throwing some on the floor, then said, "Which one? I don't see one!"

" It's light tan honey."

He moved hanger after hanger aside, saying anxiously, "Where? Where is it?"

She waddled over reached in the closet, "This one." she said.

Tony helped her with the jacket then went to the window and breathe a sigh of relief, "Thank heavens, the car is here."

"Well let's get this show on the road," she said humorously.

"How can you joke at a time like this?" he asked as he took the overnight case and started out the door.

Paige started to speak, "We'll ... Ooooooo ... " when another contraction seized her, and she had to lean against the wall puffing through the pain.

"Where is that Maggie when you really need her?" Tony asked as he supported Paige.

"Maggie is on a well deserved vacation, and I hope enjoying herself," Paige said and continued with short breaths.

"What can I do?" he asked helplessly as worry lines creased his handsome brow.

She gasped and clung to his arm, saying, "Just a minute let me get through this one then help me downstairs."

His clothes were disheveled with one coat sleeve on one arm and the other hung from the shoulder down his back. He guided her with one arm around her waist when she nodded that the pain had passed. They made their way along the hall and downstairs. Paige doubled over in pain.

Tony frantically dashed to the door and called the driver for help. They managed to get Paige into the car with Chester's help.

The drive to the hospital was slow and hectic. His love for Paige and the fact that there was nothing he could do but hold her, and coach her breathing. She rested her head on his shoulder, and gripped his sleeve.

Paige cried, "It's coming! I gotta push! I think my water broke."

"No! Not now! Listen to your coach! Blow!" he shouted, puffing, "Blow!" They reached the hospital emergency entrance as water dripped from the seat, "Chester get some help in emergency." Tony said, as the driver ran into the emergency room.

Tony carried Paige in his arms into the emergency room, and met the staff with the stretcher, he said desperately, "My wife's water broke and she is in so much pain, we are having twins!" as he laid his wife on the gurney as another contraction seized her.

"The name please?" the secretary asked.

"Ah ... ah ... Paige ah Jordan," he stammered.

A nurse covered the mother to be, and said, "I will take Mrs. Jordan to labor room one your wife has given Tammy your insurance information days ago," then pushed the stretcher toward the shadowed recesses at the end of the hall.

The secretary followed when Chester the driver brought the overnight case in and placed it under the stretcher.

"Where are you taking my wife?" Tony yelled, and started to follow.

The second nurse seeing his frustration, said with a smile, "The nurse will go along with your wife while you change into scrubs." she said soothingly, "Mr. Jordan you are just a little uneasy now, if you will come with me I'll show you to the father's changing room, and you can be with your wife in the labor room."

"I called the doctor, where is he?" Tony asked.

"Dr. Tom has already checked in he is scrubbing right now," the nurse answered.

"I don't know how to do that!" Tony protested.

The nurse gently took him by the arm, and encouraged him to go with her, "Come on I will show you the way, and help you get scrubbed and gowned," she encouraged calmly.

Reluctantly he went along, "Are you sure my wife will be all right?" he asked.

"Trust me, the doctor told us you were on the way to the hospital everything is under control, I promise." the nurse said.

Tony relaxed slightly.

And the nurse. continued soothingly, "We have to get you dressed and into the labor room with your wife then everything will be all right," as they reached the father's changing room, she sorted quickly through the scrubs, "You can change into the green scrubs and these will probably suit you. When you have changed store your clothes in this garment bag and give it to me. I will see that it goes to Mrs. Jordan's room."

Tony stuffed his clothes into the garment bag as he dressed.

"When you are changed, I want you to slip the booties over your shoes. Then use this brush and the liquid soap to scrub your hands and arms up to your elbows."

"Find out how my wife is, please." he asked.

The nurse nodded indulgently, saying, "Mrs. Jordan will be fine, Dr. Tom is here, and the nurses are with your wife. You finish washing and I will take you back, then you can be with Mrs. Jordan. Hurry, and let's get this show on the road, Dad." as he closed the wash room door.

Paige was taken from the labor room to delivery, and Tony was helping her breathe through the contractions as they seized her body every five minutes, and the last one was particularly strong. Her hospital gown was soaked with perspiration tendrils of wet hair clung to her forehead and cheeks. She breathed in short puffs as the labor progressed. Paige was tiring.

"Listen to your coach," Tony said, "slow down, slow, slow that's it breath through your discomfort then push when Dr. Tom says," as he held her in his arms in a sitting position.

After the contraction, Paige said angrily, "Tony, discomfort is a damned understatement! It hurts like hell! I'm too tired to push anymore! I want, morphine!" then leaned her full weight against her husband.

He mopped her face drying the sweat away, saying, "It's almost over, sweetheart. We've come this far and I'm here with you all the way. We agreed, no drugs."

"I lied!" she snapped.

He hugged her closer, and kissed her sweaty cheek.

Dr. Tom touched her swollen belly then listened with the stethoscope. He took his position at her feet.

He said, "That was a good contraction you 're crowning. Now I want you to push with the next one. Tony, you can help the nurse will show you how."

Tony kissed his wife, saying, "It's almost over sweetheart."

Pages eyes grew wide as she declared, "Oh, noooo here it comes, hold me Tony."

"I'm here with you, sweetheart." He said

Dr. Tom said, "Good, good here he comes, here he comes. That was great, one more good push we're almost there. On the next contraction I want you to give it all you've got," the doctor directed.

Immediately Paige tensed, crying, "Ooooo, here it comes again get the camera!" she said as she pushed with all her strength.

Tony watched in the over head mirror as the first baby was born. The circulating nurse had tried to give the camera to him but he was so fascinated with the birth he forgot the picture taking.

Tony said excitedly. "There he is! He's coming!" he laughed in awe of the miracle of birth.

"Are you getting this, poppa?" Paige asked, "There are no reruns you know."

The circulating nurse had taken the video camera and was photographing the first baby's delivery.

Dr. Tom laughed, saying comically, "This is so easy, and you're doing so well. Here comes the shoulders!" The first child was born with a lusty cry, The doctor announced, "It's a boy!"

The nurse took the new born in a sterile wrap and placed him lightly on the mothers abdomen for a short time.

The new parents were looking at their son when Paige was gripped by another strong contraction. She cried, "Ooooo Dr. Tom the other one is on his way!"

The nurse took the first son to the isolette for the pediatrician to examine

Paige sat cradled in her husband's arms breathing through the second bout of aggressive pains.

The doctor listened to the unborn child's heart beat and palpated Paige's abdomen. "Yep, it's time to get back to work," Dr. Tom said.

Tony asked, in amazement, "What! So soon!"

"Yes dad this one is in a hurry!" the doctor answered. Then he was kept busy for several minutes the second baby entered the world with a healthy shriek. "Another boy!" Dr. Tom said, placing the second enfant on his mothers abdomen.

"That was a great catch, Dr. Tom." One nurse said.

"Just call me Johnny Bench." he answered.

Then the staff shooed Tony away, saying, "You can photograph your children while we take care of Mrs. Jordan."

The mother and the children were cleaned and two nurses showed the babies to the proud parents.

Tony exclaimed, "Look sweetheart, identical twins!" He hugged her to him and kissed her, then whispered, "Thanks, Mom,"

The infants were placed in their isolette, "We'll keep your babies with us tonight, and let mom rest," one nurse explained.

In the hospital room he held Paige, saying, "We have the most wonderful boys and you, love of my life made it all possible although you did a little testy toward the end."

"Tony, I love you and the boys, but I am so tired," as she rested her head on his shoulder, saying softly, "I need a hug please. Lie with me and hold me for a while."

He climbed under the covers with Paige, "Sleep sweetheart, rest," he whispered, and stroked her back as they fell asleep together.

The grandmothers had been notified and were viewing the twins in the nursery as the babies lay warmly wrapped in their blanket cocoons.

Pat hugged Connie, saying excitedly, "Aren't they the cutest children you have ever seen?"

"No one would dare think less because they are our grand-babies," Connie answered proudly

They cooed, smiled and took pictures through the windows.

Before leaving the hospital Connie and Pat looked in on the young parents and found Tony and Paige asleep, cuddled together in the hospital bed.

Pat took a picture of the new parents as they rested, then stared at them several moments proudly, the grand-mothers crept out closing the door softly.

The morning found Tony sitting at the foot of the bed while he watched his sleeping wife as she awoke slowly, he said, "You're so beautiful when you're sleeping."

Paige laughed, and said, "Yeah, right. I am a mess, and my tongue has fuzz growing on it," as she rinsed her mouth.

Tony changed ends on the bed and hugged her tightly, "You are my mess, and I love you so much fuzz and all."

At that time the children were wheeled into the room in their separate beds.

Nurse one, said, "Mom, dad the little Jordan's are ready for breakfast, and have you decided on their names?"

In unison, they answered, "Yes."

Paige continued, "Michael Cavanaugh-Jordan was first and Mitchell Cavanaugh-Jordan is the youngest."

The nurse jotted the names on a pad then they went about showing the parents how to hold the babies, to feed and burp them.

Before leaving, nurse two said, "They are all yours now. If you need help we are only a ring away," as she closed the door.

The parents sat at either end of the bed feeding the boys listening to the television sports news.

The sportscaster, said, "In the news today ladies and gentlemen, the Anthony Jordan's are the proud parents of identical twin boys. Double or nothing folks. Tony Jordan, tennis great, bad boy of the circuits and entrepreneur of the year who owns A.J. Enterprises and Tournaments, Inc,. He has the tennis player of the year in Omar Stevenson, and many other players in transition.

The next exhibition games will be held in Canada in a matter of weeks where a number of hopefuls are scheduled to compete this young man never does anything halfway. Stay tuned for more sports and weather after this message."

"Well bad boy of the courts they should see you now," Paige said laughing.

"I think this one is full," he said, and placed the baby on his shoulder as directed then gently patted, and rubbed the infants back after a few minutes there was a moist burp. Tony said, "Oh yeah that was a good one. See that mom I've got the touch!" and grinned triumphantly.

Maggie came through the door at that time, and said, "Now where is my camera when I need it most? I never thought I would see the day Tony would be feeding a baby, and liking it. You are looking good fell a," as she went over and kissed Paige on the cheek, saying, "Hi mommy. Let me take this little bundle of delight after I have taken my gloves off. You've done enough work already," She stripped the gloves off, and used the wet wipes to clean her hands. Maggie sat in the rocker with one child. Tony turned the other over to her as well, and took pictures.

Friends and family converged on the Jordan hospital room as the babies were being taken out for the pediatrician to examine. Photographs and videos were taken of the twins behind the glass in the nursery viewing room.

The grandmothers were in the tearoom the next day.

Connie said, "Benton saw report about the twins."

"So did William, his chest stuck out a full four inches more," Pat said and laughed. "He's still a fool."

"They are so proud of them and too damn stubborn to admit it," Connie answered, "Or maybe they don't know how to give in."

"I promised to call the kids tonight. You and I will have to go shopping for little Mike and Mitch." Pat said.

"Call me after you talk to them and we will decide where to go shopping, and what to buy for kids who have everything," Connie replied, and sipped her tea.

"Will do. I brought the very first pictures here is your set," Pat said as she passed an envelope across the table.

"Oh Pat, they are so sweet," Connie said dabbing at a tear in the corner of her eye, she paused momentarily, "Now we will have to decide how they will address us."

"That's right. I am not the grandma type," Pat said.

"Neither am I that's an important matter, granny," Connie said, tongue in cheek.

They looked at each other and had a good giggle.

"Look at this shot of them together," Pat replied.

"Can't tell them apart," Connie responded.

"That's why they're called identical twins," Pat said jokingly.

"Oh you," Connie said and elbowed her friend.

"Does it make you feel aged carrying pictures of your grandchildren?" Pat asked.

"Heavens no, I have been looking forward to this since I found out about the pregnancy. This, is my badge of honor," Connie answered.

They laughed and talked in pantomime searching through their piles of photos.

Weeks later the host of Sports Round up with Jasper Guy, said, "Ladies and gentlemen we welcome to our studio tonight Anthony Jordan, one of tennis' greats. With him is Omar Stevenson the fastest rising player in the history of the game. This young man a short time ago was the find of the century, now he is heading rapidly toward first in the game. Thanks for taking time out of your busy schedules to be here."

As Tony and Omar two tall handsome young men came into sight, there was a standing ovation. Squeals from the women, whistles and shouts of encouragement from the entire audience. The guests shook hands with the host then sat across from Jasper Guy, who said, "We prepared a little pictorial for you and our audience."

In the background there were life sized photographs that appeared behind the guests. Still pictures of Tony appeared of him on the court as he fought his many battles. Then there were videos of him having a temper tantrum.

Tony covered his face partially.

Another picture of him on the town, and with his trainer.

The pictorial had the audience approval.

Jasper said, "We might as well get this question out of the way. I have to ask Tony. How did you go from being the bad boy of tennis, to entrepreneur of the year in just a few short months, and father of twins?"

Tony smiled, then responded, "The answer is not a complex one. It's taken a near death experience, a marriage made in heaven and my boys, and last but by no means least my lovely wife Paige, and this man here," he said as he squeezed Omar's shoulder, saying, "I am very fortunate."

"There has been a feud between the Jordan's and the Cavanaugh's over the years, and yet you married Paige." Jasper said.

"Yes." Tony answered.

"Your marriage was obviously against your father's wishes," Jasper said pointedly.

"Our fathers love each other, and doesn't realize it yet," Tony replied.

"How long has this feud lasted?" Jasper asked.

"Longer than I care to remember." Tony said.

"A long time," Jasper said.

"Yes, I'd say so Jasper, it's not news anymore."

"Enough said. How is your school coming along?" Jasper changed the subject.

"Better than I ever imagined," Tony replied.

"You are introducing a number of relatively new comers in Canada. Will we have some surprises?" Jasper inquired.

"I think you will have a number of surprises, especially from the juniors. I have always known the talent was here in this country. One doesn't have to go far to find the gifted one's." Tony responded.

"Anyone like Omar?" Jasper asked.

"All have Omar's potential, depends on what they want," Tony answered.

"How did you and Omar meet?"

"Actually I had seen him play on film while he was at State College. After my accident I had time on my hands, and watched all of the video footage I could find. I liked what I saw." Tony returned.

"That's right, Omar gave up the last two years at the University to go pro." Jasper recalled, then asked, "How did you persuade him to do that?"

"First there was a matter of convincing his Aunt Evelyn. She was and is a formidable woman," Tony said.

"Yes, our producers had a talk with your Aunt, this is what she showed us, ladies and gentlemen, Omar." as a life sized picture changed showing Omar the man on the tennis court, tall and straight, dressed in crisp whites and wearing a blue bandana.

The audience went wild applauding, whistling, and yelling in delight as the life sized pictures in back of Tony changed showing Omar as a toddler in diapers dragging a tennis racket, and sucking a pacifier. The baby photograph stood beside Omar the man on the tennis court.

Omar hid his face in his hand, saying, "Noooo not that picture," then the photograph changed again to Omar wearing faded blue bib over alls with the ever present bandana.

Jasper turned to Omar, saying, "I saved you 'til last to talk about your skills because you are the most prolific player I have seen in many years. How do you prepare for your matches?"

"I try to concentrate on the game at the time, and my routine is a little unorthodox. It was worked out when my Uncle Jefferson was alive. It has been my strength through the years," Omar answered.

"We have videotaped scenes coming up of you at Wimbledon," Jasper said,

The video rolled showing Omar's bold performance, the last set was a battle royal.

"A great game. How did you feel playing against Sergio?"

"I felt great. He is one of the best I've played against," Omar said in a low keyed voice.

"Tonight seems to be the time for hard questions. Omar, you participated in sit ins at the Country Club, what can you tell us about that time in your life?"

"It goes back to my childhood when my Uncle worked for the County parks system, one was near the Country Club. Sometime he would bring me to work with him, on those days I would wander over to the tennis courts at the Country Club to watch the matches. A number of times I would ask the members if I could play. The younger crowd would allow me to hit balls, and at times I participated in double matches if someone was late. I was discovered by an influential member of the board, he reported me to the manager who took me by my arm and practically dragged me to my uncle. He shouted at uncle to keep me away from the courts because I bothered the clientele, and that tennis was for whites only. I have never thought that was fair."

"The world has seen the error of their ways," Jasper said, "What are your plans now that Wimbledon is behind you?"

"Hopefully and with time, I will improve my game," Omar answered.

"If that's possible," Jasper said.

The pictures in the background changed from Tony to Omar, "There you have it ladies and gentlemen Anthony Jordan and Omar Stevenson!" audience applauded, Jasper said, "We cannot leave without mentioning Jacquelyn, the lovely lady who occupies Omar's interest off the courts," the spot light illuminated a young woman in the audience. "Give her a big hand ladies and gentlemen," as she stood to take a bow.

Omar and Tony stood to applaud.

CHAPTER 14

◆

William Jordan's study, where he turned the television off by remote control, and laughed with pride as he left the room.

Weeks later, Maggie waited for her flight along with Tony and an anxious Paige. The twins were in their tandem carriage blowing spit bubbles.

Paige said, "Maggie, you have everything Brooke's address in Europe, the tickets, diapers, ... ?"

Exasperated, Maggie answered, "I have everything I need, don't worry. I will call the second we get to Brooke's."

"The boys will be fine, dear," Tony said. "Better still why don't you go along with Mike and Mitch? I'll be there as soon as the tournaments are over."

"No," Paige answered, "I want to see the girls play, and you know I would never give up a chance to see Omar perform."

The airport paging system ask for all wheelchair passengers, then proclaimed, "Flight twelve thirty four now boarding at gate eleven."

The parents kissed the twins, and hugged Maggie.

Tony said, "Take care of my boys we'll see you in a week."

"You know I'll take care of those babies with all my cussedness if necessary." Maggie answered.

They watched Maggie push the stroller down the tunnel. She waved before she and the twins disappeared into the cavern to the plane.

"Is this the way I'll feel when they leave home in twenty years?" Paige asked.

"Probably," he answered, and hugged her shoulder as she sniffled. Then they went to the observation window and watched the plane taxi down the runway and disappear from sight.

In the air hours later in first class a passenger leaned over, and said to the twins, "Ohhh they are sooo cute just darling babies," then she reached out to touch the children.

Maggie looked up frowning, and said loudly, "Get back! Don't you dare touch these nice clean babies'!"

The woman jerked her hand away and the smile froze on her face.

Maggie continued, "Don't you even breathe in their direction, who knows what diseases you've got." as she shielded the children with a tissue.

The passenger was taken aback by the rebuff as she moved quickly to her seat with a look of embarrassment.

Maggie moved the twins off the isle to the window seat, muttering, "Breathing your filthy germs on these lovable babies," then she said sweetly, to the twins, "Don't worry my angels Maggie will keep the nasty woman away," as she buckled them in. Then she sat in the aisle seat and looked with frowning contempt at the intruder.

Stevenson smashed the last ball across the net for the game winner, and his opponent could not get in position to return it. Omar fell to his back on the ground with two thumbs up. Cheers and applause from the spectators rocked the stadium.

The announcer said, excitedly, "There you have it folks, hard fought matches by new comer's from Tennis Tournaments, Inc., of Anthony Jordan Enterprises. The father of twin boys, married to the lovely writer Paige Cavanaugh-Jordan, a man who has everything!"

Down near the tennis court, Tony and Paige were with the breathless Omar.

She hugged the tennis player, saying, "You are the very best ever, don't stop."

"I'm trying." Omar said as he shook Toney's hand then dried his face on the towel given him by the trainer.

Paige went to the group of young women players.

Tony said, "Omar, we'll meet you in Europe, after your scheduling conference. Paige and I are leaving right away. I miss my boys."

"I'll see you there," Omar answered, and went with Kirk Rodriquez.

In the cockpit of Tournaments Inc., company plane.

Night was beginning to dim the evening light. They were being plummeted by a sudden storm with gale winds and a heavy downpour.

Claude, the pilot was having problems with the static filled radio transmission, he said, into the intercom, "Mr. Jordan, would you come forward please?"

Tony came forward and sat beside the pilot, saying, "This is some storm."

"Yes, and the equipment is going haywire we are being blown off course somewhere over the Aleutians. I think we are near, Rat Island."

"I thought I saw a mountain top on the way to the cockpit," Tony said, looking at the gauges, "Our fuel is low, too."

"The radio signal is breaking up I can't raise anyone. You try," Claude responded.

Tony said into the headset, "This is LJ 1-2-8-9, do you read?" He waited the static was constant. He repeated, "This is LJ 1-2-8-9, do you read me?"

An indistinct voice broke through the static, saying, "This ... static ... Nome ... heavy static ... I can't ... static ... over."

"This is LJ 1-2-8-9 ... static ... fuel is low! ..." Tony paused, then continued, "This is LJ 1-2-8-9 we are being blown off course ... static... somewhere over ... static ... Rat Island!" static drowns the transmission.

At a small home in Seattle, in the ham radio room. Ralph Coleman a black youth who was a paraplegic, listened.

His mother, asked, "Is that plane in some kind of trouble Ralph?" as she drew up a chair to listen.

"Yes mom I've been listening, and taking notes."

"Can you help him?" she asked.

"Just a minute," he said, "I will break transmission and bring other ham operators into the crisis." as he turned to the ham radio mike, saying, "We have an emergency, all hams, please stand by." Then he turned back to the planes transmission but there was only static, and indistinct words. Ralph went to the second stand by, "To all ham operators in the proximity of this band. I'm losing the emergency signal from LJ 1-2-8-9."

The young man turned to the telephone and dialed, and waited a short time, then said, "Evan, this is Ralph. I'm calling you about a plane that's in trouble. If I'm not mistaken they were low on fuel."

"What else did you hear?" Evan asked.

"I heard, Rat Island." Ralph answered.

"In the Aleutians?" Evan asked.

"Rat Island is a part of that chain," Ralph replied.

"Thanks, I'll get right on it and call you later. Keep your ears open." Evan said.

In the cockpit of the plane, Claude yelled, "We're going down! I have to dump the fuel! Hey, you didn't .... !"

He never had the chance to finish the sentence because the plane slammed into the trees as the remaining fuel splashed to the mountainside below.

Claude and Tony were thrown against the instrument panel, and whipped around in their seats. The sounds of breaking branches, and torn metal as a tree limb smashed through the windshield, and pierced Claude's thigh, snapping the bone. The pilot screamed in agony.

Tony was conscious of Claude's cries of pain, and the cold blast of frigid air that burst through the broken windshield. Then he felt his legs being flung in the air as one knee slammed into his chin and he tasted the salt of his own blood.

The plane skidded forward on the rocky ground tearing small trees and shrubs up by the roots, scattering rocks and boulders, leaving chunks of metal in its path.

As the plane plowed across the mountainside they were tossed forward again when the plane came to an abrupt stop. Pain shot through Toney's chest. When he recovered somewhat he helped Claude to the floor of the cockpit, and the searing pain gripped his chest again

Paige's screams filters into his dazed mind. He groped his way to the passengers section, wiping the blood from his mouth and chin.

When he tried to unbuckle his wife's seat belt the whole restraint section came away in his hand. It had been torn away from the seat housing. Her face was awash with blood from her forehead where she had been thrown into the seat opposite. She sat holding her groggy head.

Tony laid Paige on the floor then went for the first aid kit and was back quickly to stem the bleeding, and clean the cut over her eye. He had finished when she begun to regain lucidity.

"Are you all right? Anything broken?" he asked, as he checked her legs, arms and body, and found no other obvious injuries.

"I think so but you're favoring your side, let me see," Paige said lifting his shirt to reveal an angry reddened area over his ribs.

He flinched away when she touched the spot.

She continued, saying, "Your ribs are badly bruised, or fractured. I need something to bind them," she searched in the rear of the plane and found ace bandages then wound them around his rib cage.

"That feels better, I don't think they're broken, I'm not having difficulty breathing," Tony said as he gingerly moved his upper body, then said, "Claude is in bad shape, we have to bring him in here. Do you think you can help?" he asked.

She nodded.

"After that we need to check our supplies and other options then find shelter from the wind tonight. It is only by the miracle of fate that we are all alive," Tony said.

They had to drag Claude screaming in agony from the cockpit as they struggled and stumbled over debris in the failing light.

"We will take him to the rear and lay him on the carpet." Tony said, out of breath.

The pilot was suffering as he stared blankly at them then settled into unconsciousness.

Tony continued, "Honey, look in the locker in the back, there are flashlights and more bandages bring them, we have to do something about that small limb imbedded in his thigh," then he bent down and tore the pilots blood soaked pants leg open up to his groin.

Paige brought the flashlights and anything for a make shift bandage and had a better look at the horrid wound. Paige helped to hold Claude as Tony worked the small limb out of his thigh leaving a gaping tear in the flesh. The pilot bellowed once and fought weakly throughout the ordeal then passed out again.

Tony cleaned and packed the wound with a part of a clean towel then bound the leg snugly with Paige's help, he said, "The break seems clean, and it's good he is unconscious. It would have been hell to pay if he had been more awake through it all." as he surveyed his handy-work, "Honey, bring more ace bandages."

Paige scurried to the back of the plane and was back soon.

Tony said, "This magazine splint will have to do until morning." he paused and turned to hold Paige, saying, "The radio is out we'll have to walk off this mountain. Are you game?"

"Wouldn't miss it for the world," she answered.

"That's my girl. When it's daylight we have to see what our supplies are. Now we need rest and to get through the night."

They gathered coverings, pillows and tucked Claude in. Then snuggled together for warmth behind seats to shield them from the bone chilling wind.

Benton and Connie were watching the telecast when, the announcer said, "Anthony and Paige Jordan's last transmission was heard over the Aleutian Islands. Luckily their children were with Maggie, the nanny in Europe. The parent's were on their way to join them at the vacation home of Brooke Topplinger's. Stay tuned for further development in this tragic incident, and now this ... "

Benton turned the television off by remote control then left the room shaken. He went directly to the telephone in the pantry and dialed a number, he said, "This is Benton Cavanaugh, you saw the news?"

"Yes, sir."

"I want you to take my plane and find that island where they crashed. Find my daughter, and Anthony her husband. Understand?" Benton ordered.

In the Jordan home the same scenario was taking place.

William said, "Take the Lear jet, and find them!" then slammed the receiver down, and sat disheartened.

Connie's dressing room, she said, "Pat, did you hear that awful news?"

"Yes, I'm already packed I'm leaving tonight we have to take care of our grand babies. Flight plans are being made as we speak," Pat answered.

"I will be ready pick me up on the way," Connie said, as she hurriedly threw the bare necessities into a bag.

Benton stepped into the hall as Connie came down stairs carrying a bag.

He asked, "Where are you going?"

"To see about my children," she answered.

"But I ... I" Benton bristled.

"Forbid all you want I'm going tonight!" Connie interrupted brusquely.

"She's not our responsibility, and ..."

Connie stopped him in mid-sentence, saying coldly, "Don't even go there Benton don't you dare. You don't speak for me! Paige is our daughter and I'm going to see about her and Tony, and my grand-babies!"

"You would defy me?" Benton sputtered.

"Then you live with it Benton. I repeat, she's our daughter and don't you dare try to forget that!"

The doorbell rang and Connie went to answer with her bag. Pat was about to ring again as Connie opened the door, saying, "I'm ready, Pat."

"Good-bye Benton." Patricia said.

He stood at a loss for words then finally managed to say, "Connie I need ... " he said helplessly.

She turned, saying, "You know where I will be Benton, Brooke's address is on my vanity if you care to look." as she climbed into the limousine after Pat.

The grand-mother's were parked on the Jordan private air-strip alongside the company Jet.

William protested, saying, "If you go you won't take this plane!"

"And who is stopping me?" Pat asked defiantly.

William turned to the pilot, and ordered, "Bernhard, you won't be needed."

Patricia was fuming, then asked, "Bernhard, who hired you, and the co-pilot?"

The pilot was caught in a sticky situation, answered, "Your father, ma'am."

"Enough said, I can fly the damn thing myself. Did you file the flight plan as I, instructed you to do?" Pat asked pointedly.

"Yes, ma'am," Bernhard answered.

"Well get on board man we're wasting precious time standing here arguing." Pat said, and turned to her husband, "William, you know where I will be."

"I won't call!" he barked.

"So be it. Come, Connie times wasting,"

The women climbed aboard the aircraft. The plane taxied along the runway, gained speed and flew into the darkened sky.

CHAPTER 15

◆

The rain had stopped and the wind was less brisk as the first light of day filtered through the trees over the mountain top.

Tony awoke tiredly because he and Paige had not truly slept but shifted between a dream like state and the realization that they had been in a plane crash. They assessed their situation, and found the plane had skidded into a gash in the mountain. The cockpit was caught and held there dangerously clinging on the edge of a steep cliff on one side of the crevasse, and by that miracle of fate they had been saved. The rear of the plane had been torn partially from the cockpit as it rested on a cushion of jagged shrubs.

Claude moaned and tried to sit upright when a sharp pain shot through his leg. He cried out with agony and fell back on the blanket. The hair on his forehead was matted with congealed blood and dried smaller clots clung to his eyebrows. His chest wound was bound snugly and the bandage was clear of fresh bleeding. Another wave of pain and nausea swept over the pilot. He closed his eyes and blacked out for several minutes.

Paige said, "I found some pain killers but we will have to use them with care. I'll give two to Claude when he's awake."

Tony stood near the edge of the cliff looking through binoculars, saying, "I can see smoke curling toward the clouds in the distance to the east of here." He gave the glasses to Paige and pointed in the direction of the smoke as he massaged her back gently.

"That looks so far away, and I am so cold!" she answered.

"We'll make it, "he whispered, "Come over here. I found dry wood for a fire, and food along with a warmer coat for you," as he helped her on with the long coat. "We need to eat to keep up our strength," then he led her from the clearing, "We can sit by the fire away from the wind then I want to look at your wounds and bandages."

"Why can't we sleep inside the plane?" she asked.

"I'm afraid a strong gust of wind will blow what's left of the plane out of that crack and we would go tumbling down the mountain to oblivion." Tony answered.

"Perish that thought. I was asleep when we crashed. I thought we were having an earthquake," Paige said as she followed him to the shelter of the trees.

Tony examined her wounds making sure her injuries were minor then rubbed his chest flexing his muscles, saying, "I don't think my ribs are broken probably just badly bruised. The pain is less this morning especially when I draw a deep breath. We will need to forage for more fire wood after we have eaten. Then we need to find something suitable to devise a litter for Claude. We can't leave him here he would never survive,"

He stood to swing his arms to warm up, when he spoke little puffs of vapor followed his words.

They walked along the swatch of fallen trees the plane had leveled. There were deep gouges across the slope where the plane had skidded tearing up chunks of earth leaving twisted metal along the way. At the edge of the cliff they found a manageable precipice of gooey mud that marked the nearest gullies as the wind whipped the branches of the trees.

"How did you become so smart about the great outdoors?" she asked.

"I spent some time in the Sierras." he answered.

The wind began to howl through the trees.

Paige felt the skin around her nose and cheek. The swelling was there along with a blood shot eye, she cried, "I've got a black eye!"

"The cutest little shiner I have ever seen," he laughed, and smoothed the hair from her face, then whispered, "I love you, this face we can live with you look great to me. It wounds me that you were hurt at all. I couldn't bare it if your injury had been worse," he touched his lips to hers.

"I need a hug please," Paige said, and he enfolded her in his arms. She laid her head gently on his chest, saying, "You have good taste and your eye sight is impeccable, and I love you madly."

"You should have stayed with the boys you would be safe now." Tony answered.

"I would be worried sick about you, we are a team. I am here to take care of you," Paige said.

Tony kissed her, and said, "I've gotta get busy."

Tony and Paige climbed into the plane and he began tossing supplies down to Paige. Soon a pile of usable goods lay on the ground blankets, a sleeping bag, food and a bottle of brandy, first aid kit, a rain coat and sweats.

In the cabin of the plane Tony pulled at the cables and doubled over in pain when he forgot his damaged ribs and pulled too hard. As the discomfort subsided he went back to the task of removing the cable and wiring. When he had finished he had coils of wire and cables and dropped it to the ground. Later he found several bottles of water and precious matches.

The wrecked plane creaked loudly and lurched as a part of the wing tore off and fell crashing into the gorge below after a strong gust of wind swirled through the cavity of the downed aircraft.

Paige was busy separating the articles and carrying them to the wooded area. She screamed, "Tony!"

"I'm all right, I have about all I will need from here, I'll throw it down," he yelled.

"Tony, hurry we can't have you falling into the ravine." she said.

He had finished tossing everything he had collected to the ground, when the down plane groaned savagely under the strong winds and the wreck shifted position drastically as tearing metal screeched piercingly. Tony was forced to jump and rolled free of the falling rubble as he held his chest.

Paige ran to him and helped him to his feet, as they ran to the shelter of the trees the wind shifted and the plane rolled toward them, she cried, "Oh sweetheart are you all right? Please, don't go in there again, I see what you meant about the danger." as she hugged him, he winced with the pain, she said, "Oh Tony, sweetheart did I hurt you?"

"I landed in an awkward position just give me a minute," as he deep breathed.

"Can I get you a pain pill?" she asked.

Tony held her, and said, "No, this will go away soon, we'll need the pills later. We don't need anything else out of there but you should stay behind the shelter of the trees because the wind could shift this way suddenly. I'll be right back."

"Are you sure you are all right?" she asked.

"I am fine," then he kissed her lightly on the lips and walked into the wooded area favoring his side. After a while he came back with two poles, and other wood.

"What are you doing?" Paige asked.

"I am putting together a stretcher to carry Claude, and a shelter for us tonight." Tony answered,

"Can I help?" Paige asked.

"Yes, find food for us and make a small fire, those larger scrapes of metal will shield the fire and us."

"I can do that." she said.

"We'll shoot one of the flares when it's dark enough. Tomorrow we have to walk off this mountain. We can't survive here for any length of time. Claude's condition is grave."

On a commercial jet liner in first class, William slowly walked down the aisle looking for his seat. Ironically he was seated beside Benton who tried to hide his face behind his hat.

"Imagine meeting you here, Benton." William said.

Benton folded his arms and didn't answer but made an unintelligible noise then looked the other way.

William continued, "And, you are wearing a hat. Pardon me if I don't shake hands."

Benton faced his adversary, asking grumpily, "What are you doing here?"

"I will give you two guesses," William replied.

"I'll get another seat, oh miss ... " he said, and stood trying to signal the flight attendant with one forefinger in the air.

"Don't be a bigger ass than you already are, sit down," William responded.

"You can't talk to me like that!" Benton said, in a loud whisper.

"I can and will. You were a jerk in school, and you're a bigger one now," William shot back.

"I was, not! Besides who put a stamp on your ass and said you were perfect?" Benton said indignantly.

"Benton, calm down we both know why we are here," William's words had a sobering effect.

Benton stopped and sat slowly down with a sigh, saying, "Yes, you're right. Do you think they're okay?"

"Heavens, I hope so," was William's quiet response, "Maybe our wives are smarter than we give them credit for."

"You may be right there, Connie gave me hell for the first time in a long time," Benton said.

They sat silently in worried thought.

Early the next morning on the mountain in the Aleutians, cold winds whipped the trees.

Claude was awake and nibbled a small amount of food and drank the hot sweet tea.

Tony asked, "Claude how is the leg?"

"Not so bad, I think it's a clean break but I have the damnedest headache," Claude replied.

Paige gave him two pain killers then gathered the packed supplies and passed out the matches. She said, "You should keep the matches in an inside pocket where they won't get wet."

Tony was struggling to get into the heavy coat he had found on the plane. he said, "Let's get started. If we are going to do this the sooner the better."

Paige tucked the blankets around Claude, saying, "Is this all we are taking?" she asked, then walked over to check Toney's rib dressing before he fastened his coat. "Do you have enough support and padding? Your bindings seem okay."

"We can't carry anymore, and I have enough padding stop worrying we are going to make it," Tony said, then pulled her into his arms, saying softly, "You have a lot to carry will you be able to manage the double sleeping bag?"

"Yes, as long as I'm with you. If I remember correctly you tried to talk me out of all this fun." Paige said as she rested her head on his shoulder momentarily.

"You could leave me." Claude said.

"No, we can't do that besides I may not be able to find this place again," Tony replied.

"Perish that thought. We could make a walking splint. I would handle that on my own," Claude said.

"You can't bare weight on that leg you could lose it," Tony said and held up a bottle, asking, "Claude, how do you like you brandy?"

"In a cup," the pilot replied.

Tony brought the paper cup of liquor and waited for him to drink. He had a good look at Claude. The pilots eyes were sunken with dark circles and a ghastly pallor under his facial bruises.

Then Tony strapped the pilot to the make shift litter, saying, "I'll tuck the flare gun and flares under your blanket." He tied a rag around his head as a sweat band then shrugged into the harness and pulled the stretcher to the best way down the slope.

Winds howled through the trees slowing their progress as they trudged down the grade.

In the afternoon they had made reasonable progress.

Paige went ahead and stepped on a loose shelf of gravel. Her weight sent a shower of rocks cascading down the incline as she tumbled several yards down the hill. The heavy back pack dragged and caught on the shrubs slowing her plunge to the ledge below.

Tony yelled, "Paige!" as she disappeared from sight down the slope. He hurriedly shed his harness and ran to help her.

She sat up holding her head bleeding from a gash over her eyes, and said, "Oh my head that was some fall."

"Here let me see that." Tony said, "That's a nasty cut. Come over here against the cliff. I'll put a bandage on the cut," he retrieved the first aid kit and cleaned the laceration with a little brandy.

"Ouch, that hurts," she said, as she flinched away.

"Can you go on would you like to stop?" Tony asked.

"Yes we go on I'm fine, I have a hard head." She answered.

Claude shivered from the cold, his infection, and growing delirium. shouted, "I'm coming! Wait don't go!"

Tony bellowed, "Claude! Don't move!" as he ran up the slope to calm the pilot, and check his bindings.

"I'll keep an eye on him. How are your ribs?" Paige asked as she followed him.

"My ribs are okay but I'm worried about you, are you sure you can go on?" he asked.

"Yes I'm all right, sweetheart," she answered.

"I need to scout ahead for a place to camp tonight," Tony said, "Give Claude a painkiller with a little brandy that should hold him. I'll be back as soon as possible," he went into the wood ahead.

The uneven ground was on a downward slope and almost impossible to navigate with the load they had to carry. Tony was exhausted and needed to rest but they had to have shelter from the cold wind . He came out above a sheer rock slide area where rocks crashed to the bottom. A short distant ahead there seem to be a better place for them to camp. He explored the area to make sure the ground was not a slide area.

Satisfied Tony went back to Paige and Claude, saying. "If we go on for another two hundred yards there is a plateau. At the bottom of the cliff is a better place for us to camp tonight. There is more shelter from the wind than on the mountainside and plenty of firewood." Tony tested the pilots bindings, the pain pills and brandy seemed to be working. Then he shrugged into his harness to the litter and started to drag it forward.

When they reached the selected spot, Paige massaged his back.

Tony said, "I'll have to rest a moment then I will lower you first and then Claude. We can use some hot food for warmth and to rebuild our strength. After dark we'll fire another flare."

"I'll gather the wood for the fire when we're down." Paige said.

Claude yelled suddenly, "Get him! Don't dive! Don't dive! The water is too deep! No! No! No!" He shouted and laughed maniacally. Then he whispered feverishly, "I got you buddy. It's all right," his whispers continued incoherently along with intermittent shivering.

"How are we doing with the pain pills and brandy?" Tony asked.

"We have to go easy on them both the pills were never intended for his kind of pain. The medicine never seems to last long but the brandy helps." she answered.

Tony closed the cap on the water bottle and tucked it inside her pack, saying, "Are you ready?"

"Yep. I'm ready. Claude is so restless we'll have to make sure his bindings are secure. While you do that I'll drop all the packs over first." Paige said.

"Are you sure you're up to this?" he asked.

She nodded her head as he tied the cable around her waist and looped one end around a tree, he asked again, "You're sure? Claude is quite heavy," Tony hugged her gently and her arms were around him.

"Sweetheart, I will be all right besides we're almost at the bottom. I like the idea of not having to slide down anymore cliffs tomorrow morning."

"Okay. let's get started," he said and lowered her slowly over the edge as loose gravel showered to the ground below. When she was safely down Paige untied the cable. Tony pulled it up and secured Claude to the stretcher with more torn strips of blanket around his chest, abdomen and legs then started to let him down. At the half way point Claude started to rave, and in his delirium struggled to free himself. His body started to slip off the end as the stretcher twisted grotesquely. just as the pilot was near the bottom his body slipped out the end of the ties and fell head first landing on a bed of limbs opening a cut.

Tony watched helplessly.

Paige rolled Claude over on his back, the pilot screamed in pain. She had to fight to hold him down when she release the line for Tony then she fought to apply pressure to the cut. The pilot yelled and flayed his arms whilst his body shivered violently.

Tony repelled down quickly to help Paige contain the pilot.

They gathered wood and built a roaring fire then unpacked two small pots for heating food and water for tea from their meager larder. After they had eaten Paige managed to get warm sweet tea and brandy between Claude's parched lips along with the pain pills.

"We'll move him over to the foot of the trees, and secure him to one of the sapling," Tony said, as they tucked the blankets securely retying the strips of blanket.

Paige spread the double sleeping bag nearby, and said, "Don't forget the flare, sweetheart."

He stood tiredly and found the flare gun where Claude had fallen and shot the flare into the night. At last he crawled into the sleeping bag with Paige.

They didn't sleep during the night but seemed to move between slumber and unconsciousness. Always aware of Claude's screams as he ranted and raved incoherently through the night, his ranting always involved his time as a pilot in combat.

The air was frigid at the bottom of the mountain as daylight dawned, the sun rose brilliantly over the trees and shrubs.

Tony awoke as Paige was feeding the fire and boiling water. She gave him a hot cup of tea, saying, "Claude settled down a little while ago. Tony we're almost out of pain pills and his leg dressing need to be changed. It's starting to smell."

"I'll change it, and we have to get him to a doctor as soon as possible somehow." Tony answered, then searched through the meager supplies for bandages and removed the old dressing as blood and pus flowed from the malodorous purple wound. He cleansed the lesion and poured some of the precious brandy into the cavity then repacked it.

Claude didn't cry out or move, "After we eat we need to get started, how is our water supply," Tony asked.

"Two bottles of water left very few bandages, nine pain pills, two packs of matches and this is the last of the brandy," Paige said holding up the bottle, "And miles to go before we sleep." she added.

Tony went to her, and said softly, "We need a hug, and we will get through this all right," as he enfolded her in his arms.

Paige embraced him with her head on his chest they seemed to gain strength from their touch.

CHAPTER 16

◆

Ralph Coleman, operating under his ham radio call letters was talking to another operator, he said, "Thomas, this is Ralph in Seattle. Over."

There were a few crackles and, a voice answered, "Hey Ralph, you're up early what's happening? Over."

"Did you get a transmission four nights ago involving a private plane that crashed on, or about Rat Island? Over." Ralph asked.

"Can you be more specific? Over."

"I did some checking and I figure it's near Mt. Katmai in your neck of the woods. Over."

"There was a storm about that time. One of my kids said he saw a light in the sky. Over."

"That might have been their signal,. Over." Ralph suggested.

"You know how kids are always seeing something, asking questions. I thought they saw lightening. Over."

"Can you check it out? Over." Ralph asked.

"We will have to go through the tall grass, wet and messy after a storm. We'll have a look at first light, "I'll get back to you, over and out." Thomas said as he signed off.

At the base of the mountain the survivors were breaking camp, and about to descend into the tall grass.

Tony said, "I think we should head toward the mountain peak where we saw the smoke.." He held Paige then checked Claude's bindings.

Before struggling into his coat over the thick padding and zipped it closed then shrugged into the harness. Tony dragged his burden into the tall grass as

Paige made a path.

The going was painfully slow from the start because the grass was wet and pulled at their clothes, the stretcher and any other thing they were carrying.

When the sun reached its pinnacle at mid-day they had gone only a few miles.

Claude had not regained consciousness but shivers shook his body violently.

Tony and Paige were beyond exhaustion.

He said, "We'll have to rest a while my pelvis is aching from that old tennis injury, pulling the litter has aggravated it."

"Have some water and a little brandy to help you relax," Paige said.

They shared the water then laid down together on the open sleeping bag and was instantly asleep.

Five Aleutian men came upon the exhausted trio. They examined the make shift camp.

One asked, "Is that a woman?"

"Yep, that one is a woman." Thomas said.

Tony awoke, shook Paige, saying, "We have company," She rolled over to see the men staring down at them. Tony said, "Hello."

Thomas was examining the stretcher, he asked, "You did this yourself?"

"Yes." Tony answered.

"Good job. I am Thomas and we will help you back to our village. This man is in bad shape," he said.

"Do you have a telephone?" Tony asked.

"No telephone we have ham radio sets," Thomas answered.

"Great! Just great!" Tony replied with relief.

Thomas said, "Just follow us."

The villagers took the litter and their equipment and walked easily through the grass.

Paige said, "I don't think I could have gone on much longer."

"Yes I know. Claude needs medical attention badly," Tony said as they followed tiredly. The winds whipped the grass viciously

When they reached Thomas' house in the village his wife met them at the door, saying, "You must be the Jordan's. Come in there is hot coffee and food to warm you."

"Could we talk to the ham radio operator? Claude, our pilot needs attention right away." Tony asked.

"You are in the right place, I am the operator," Thomas answered.

"I don't want to rush you but he is my first priority," Tony said.

"No problem, we will do it now but first my wife, Mercedes will show Mrs. Jordan where to wash up you both could use some attention, too. Our doctor will have a look at you and your wife later," Thomas beckoned Tony to follow him.

Paige said, "The shower is for me lead me to it please," and followed Mercedes from the room.

Thomas poured hot coffee then turned on the ham radio set, saying, "A ham operator named Ralph Coleman told me about your plane crash this morning. That's why we were looking for your party," an intercom system buzzed, Thomas listened then hung up the receiver, and said, "Your pilots conditions can be stabilized, he is suffering from infection and exposure. Our doctor has his pain under control and will give him an antibiotic, and fluids now. Any allergies we should know about"

"I can't remember any." Tony said.

"The patient will be going to the hospital in the next town for more extensive treatment. The Med-E-Vac unit will be here soon."

"I'm glad you found us when you did, my wife was worn and so tired. Could I talk to the ham operator?" Tony asked.

"The set should be ready," Thomas turned to the set, talking all the time, "Ralph is paraplegic an African American teenager always tapping out Morse code when he's not gabbing. It was Ralph who figured the general vicinity of where your plane went down, smart kid," as he worked with the dials. "I will have him in a few seconds. I'm using a phase patch and you can speak directly to him." Thomas tinkered with the receiver and soon had Ralph on the line, he said, "Ralph? Thomas. we found them almost exactly where your calculation suggested. Here is Mr. Jordan, he would like to speak to you. Over."

Tony took the receiver, "Hello Ralph, I understand we have you to thank for our rescue this morning, Over."

"I reported your transmission are you and your party all right? Over"

"Claude, our pilot is in bad shape, Over." Tony said.

"When I called Thomas this morning I was hoping they would find you. Over."

"You were right on the money our plane went down on Mt. Katmai. Over."

"You're in Thomas' village, that's good. Over."

"Yes, we are a few miles north of the Valley of Ten Thousand Smokes. Ralph, I have one more favor."

"Fire away. Over," Ralph said.

"Would you contact this number 818-879-4992, and tell Kenneth Bellingham where we are and he will arrange everything from there, Over."

"I will report your location and help will be on the way shortly. Tell Thomas I will contact him later, Over and out."

Ham operators cross all social and economic boundaries. Their homes are top heavy with massive antenna towers. They spend nights and weekends tapping out Morse code, and talking to people all over the world. The common tie that pulls them together everywhere is the desire to be on the air.

In Brooke's European Villa family and friends were gathered around the television set when the newscaster said, "The Jordan party was rescued only hours ago. Their injuries were not life threatening. The miraculous feat was the tenacity it took for Anthony Jordan in spite of an old tennis injury, bruised ribs along with the help of his lovely wife to literally drag the handmade litter down the mountain and through tall wet grass before being rescued."

In the background and to the side of the newsman, a med-e-van unit waited. Claude was being lifted into the aircraft.

The news, continued, "Claude, the Jordan pilot has a fractured leg, shattered shoulder and multiple lacerations and contusions, all are suffering from exposure. If it had not been for a teenage ham radio operator in Seattle named Ralph Coleman. The rescue may have taken longer. We will follow this feat of heroism as the news unfolds."

His co-anchor, said, "That was a nice touch people helping people."

Brooke's guests hugged one another happily. The grandfathers slapped each other on the back.

"There they go! Look at that!" they watched as the plane lifted off smoothly.

Connie said, to one baby, "Did you see your mommy and daddy? They are coming home, sweetheart."

Pat held the other child up, saying, "Yes, they are and you're such a good baby." as she hugged the infant to her bosom.

The twins grinned toothlessly making gurgling noises, loving all the attention.

The news media converged on Ralph Coleman's lawn and porch. The mayor along with Ralph's mother were surrounded by the press.

Mayor Schiff said, in his best political voice, "We are gathered here today to present this commendation to Ralph Coleman for his quick thinking in the rescue of the Jordan party. As you know it was Ralph's calculations that lead his friend Thomas Ponchnix to the crash victims, days sooner than anticipated." Mayor Schiff turned to Ralph, saying, "Ralph, on behalf of the city of Seattle and its citizens I present to you this metal for your assistance in a time of difficulty."

One reporter with a cellular telephone, shouted, "Ralph, we have someone on the line who wants to speak with you." he pressed a button.

Toney's voice spilled out, he said, "Ralph, Paige and I wish we could be there today but we haven't been released from the hospital yet."

Paige said, "We will be looking forward to meeting you personally to thank you properly for our lives. If ever there was a hero, you're mine Ralph." She still wore a small bandage over one eye.

"Thanks, it was a piece of cake," Ralph answered, "How is Claude?"

"His leg was saved, and he seems to be getting better after his ordeal. Claude is still a little disgruntle and swears we dropped him on his head on purpose.

My wife and I wanted to thank you, and we will see you soon. Is there anything you would like?"

"To meet Omar Stevenson, and see him play in person." he answered.

"Consider it done." Tony said.

The mayor shook Ralph's hand again and then his mother's as the photographers flash bulbs lit up the front porch.

In the afternoon four days later Tony and Paige arrived at Brooke's European home.

Brooke and her guests could be seen near the pool.

Clive let them into the house, saying with a lisp, "I'm so glad you guys are all right come on in here. The twins are asleep upstairs with Maggie. Go girl, I'll tell everybody you are here."

Paige hugged Clive before they ran upstairs.

They were cuddling the twins. While Maggie stood in the doorway, watching, she said, "I knew you would be all right I'm glad you're back, and you're late by several days."

Tony crossed to her and embraced her with one arm, saying, "We tried our best. Thanks for taking care of the boys."

Paige had followed and kissed her on the cheek.

"I didn't have to do much," Maggie answered, "With the grand-parents around, and those grand-fathers are the worse."

The boys gurgled, and drooled happily as their parents took them downstairs. When they reached the living room the grandmothers followed by the whole group of friends came inside.

The well wishers clamored their pleasure with their return.

The mothers embraced their grown children then stood back to get a better look, when they were satisfied they were all right they took the grand babies.

William and Benton arrived from a different part of the house, and went to their children.

"I am glad you are safe," William said, as he leaned back, saying, "I thought I told you no more close calls."

"Close call wasn't in my plan this was an act of, God." Tony said laughing.

"You're home safe and sound that's all that counts," Benton said, with solemn emotions as he held Paige at arm's length then took her in his arms and rocked her.

William tapped Benton on the shoulder, and said,

It's my turn to talk now," then smiled down at Paige, "Twins yet." He folded her in his arms as she hugged him around the midsection. "You'll have to go by ship next time something safe."

Maggie said, "Remember the Titanic?"

Brooke smiled, saying, "Maggie the party pooper."

Benton shook Tony's hand then hugged him, and said, "It's a little late but welcome to the family."

"Thanks, the pleasure is all mine," Tony answered.

"I appreciate your taking care of my baby," Benton said.

"What can I say, I love her," Tony responded.

"You and my daughter seem in good health to me, Mike and Mitch needs us now." Benton said.

The amenities over the grand-fathers took the twins. William said, "They look at lot like my side of the family."

"Where did you get that notion?" Benton asked, as they walked toward the door.

The babies stared from one to the other in wonder.

The people assembled watched and laughed knowingly.

Maggie said, "See, what did I tell you?"

William answered, "The eyes, the shape of their heads, a known sign of intelligence good Jordan stock."

"The Cavanaugh intellect it's as plain as the nose on your face." Benton retorted.

"Anyone with eyes can see these beautiful children are Jordan's!" William said as they left the room.

Maggie laughed, saying, "What can I say. They are hooked," as she plopped down in a chair.

Webster's dictionary defines grand as illustrious, distinguished, imposing, noble, dignified, indicative of family relations of the ninth degree.

It was decided long ago that God couldn't be everywhere at once so he created grand-parents

Although not quite like these, tall, old fashioned, pompous, and argumentative grand-fathers.

EPILOGUE

◆

A television newscaster in Williams office weeks later, said, "There was a merger of Jordan Industries, with Cavanaugh the Conglomerate to form Cava-Jar Corporation, Inc."

The flash bulbs flared.

"Well folks, it has been said as we live our lives there is always room for love to get better. The feuding was ended by twin boys. You know the story, and a child shall lead us."

The camera showed a picture of the grandfathers standing proudly behind the desk. The twins sat in a duel baby seat atop the desk with toothless grins, kicking, bouncing, drooling and blowing spit bubbles.

Tony and Paige watched the broadcast.

She said, softly, "This makes everything alright, and I love you more and more every day," as she leaned her head on his shoulder.

"You know that goes double for me. I'm completely and unconditionally bewitched by you," he said as he embraced Paige.

"We may never see our kids again," she said contentedly.

"You may be right we may have two budding businessmen on our hands besides we can always make some more." He said. as the television screen went to black.

"We could do that because you make me glow," Paige said, seductively, "Let's have some music, I want to dance with you up close. an personal."

"This all started with a dance," Tony whispered.

"Yes, it did," Paige giggled.

The music surrounded them as they enfolded each other in their arms, and swayed to the music aware of every point of touch.

Paige wore the top and he wore the bottoms to the sweats..

THE END.